THE
LEGEND
OF THE
DIVINE
CALENDAR

THE LEGEND OF THE DIVINE CALENDAR

NOVELLA ONE

FATHER ELISHA

FATHER ELISHA

THE LEGEND OF THE DIVINE CALENDAR

Copyright © 2024 Father Elisha
Published in June 2024 by Father Elisha
Phoenix, Arizona, USA,
Website: fatherelisha.com
Email: hello@fatherelisha.com

Cover design by Elishewa and Jonathan Rhein.
Interior design by Father Elisha.

All rights reserved. No part of this publication may be translated, reproduced, stored in a retrieval system, or transmitted in any form or by any means— electronic, mechanical, photocopy, recording, or otherwise—without the prior written permission of Father Elisha.

This novella is a work of fiction. Names, characters, places, and incidents either are the product of the author's imagination or are used fictitiously. Any resemblance to actual events, locales, organizations, or persons living or dead is entirely coincidental and beyond the intent of either the author or publisher.

Except for the cover and interior design, all content in this publication was created without the use of artificial intelligence (AI) technology. All writing, editing, and creative processes were conducted by human authors and contributors.

Scripture quotations are taken from the New King James Version ®.
Copyright © 1982 by Thomas Nelson. Used by permission.
All rights reserved.

ISBN: 979-8-9906922-0-6 (paperback)

To Jesus Christ, I owe You everything.

To my sister, Anette, and her family.

And to the monks in my monastery,
Rafael, Michael, Joseph, David, and Michael.
You are gifts from the Heavenly Father to me.

CONTENTS

Chapter 1: Freedom Adventures 1

Chapter 2: Wounded 13

Chapter 3: The Divine Calendar 27

Chapter 4: The Map of the Kingdom 41

Chapter 5: Anywhere but Utah 53

Chapter 6: Heavenly Blueprints 63

Chapter 7: The Chosen Steward 75

Chapter 8: Furious Jesus 89

Chapter 9: First Symbol 101

Chapter 10: The Race: First Lap 117

Chapter 11: The Race: Second Lap 129

Chapter 12: The Race: Final Lap 145

Chapter 13: Zeal for Your House 155

Chapter 14: Man of Responsibility 165

Epilogue: New Beginning 183

Acknowledgments 199

Author's Note 201

About the Author 203

"Do not neglect the gift that is in you, which was given to you by prophecy with the laying on of the hands of the eldership."

1 TIMOTHY 4:14

Chapter 1

FREEDOM ADVENTURES

Valley of the Gods, Utah, Sunday, July 26, 2020

Sand bounced off Leo's helmet visor as he speeded his Polaris terrain vehicle down the canyon's winding road. "I can't believe Mom said that, bro! And *no*, I'm *not* talking to her! You understand me, so you talk to her."

As he approached a tight turn, he fought with the phone call's volume control. "Man, that's not true! I helped her and everyone all week! This is my time and this day isn't over. Where I'm going is none of her business. She isn't that militant about you, you know. I'm an adult. It's not like she owns me—whoa!"

Leo slid toward a Jeep coming the other way, and his backpack flew out, scattering his climbing gear on the road.

"Stop!" Leo roared at his off-roader.

He skated the pebbles and cranked the wheel, skidding toward the Jeep's side. Gritting his teeth and closing his eyes, Leo braced himself.

A screeching thud, and the seatbelt caught him. Beyond the whir of the radiator fans, a terrible silence magnified his blunder. His heart pounding, he grasped for the empty passenger seat. Sand ticked on the metal as the tailing dust cloud invaded Leo's side-by-side. He still had the brake pressed to the floor but couldn't bring himself to release it.

To his left was a dented *Way To Go! Counseling* logo, and above it, a tattooed, bald man with an elaborately curled orange mustache stared down at him. Behind the white knuckles gripping the Jeep's wheel, gawked an elderly man. The driver tried to open the door, but Leo's Polaris blocked him. The stern face turned red, a vein bulging in the forehead.

"Leo?!" his brother said in his earphones. "What's going on? Say something, will ya?"

"Talk to you later, brother." Leo hung up.

The Jeep's window rolled down. "Maniac! Where did you learn to drive?!"

He squeezed the steering wheel, knowing his helmet hid his face. Would the Polaris start?

"Back up!" The door slammed into Leo's vehicle until the roll cage vibrated. "We're going to sort this out right now!"

"Fred," the old man said. "Sho' 'nuff this here was an accident."

Leo mentally listed everything in his backpack. Apart from the climbing equipment, nothing could identify him. He turned the ignition and the engine started.

Fred's stare struck his temple like lightning. "Don't you dare! . . ."

Leo was sure of one thing: He was not stepping out. Except for crumpling the Jeep's door and giving them the shock of their week—there was no serious harm. Sissy or not, he was getting out of there.

He threw the Polaris into reverse and spun backward. The man covered his face, cursing him as the dust rose. Quickly, Leo turned the wheel and braked. The vehicle slid to a halt, blocking the road.

From within the dust cloud, Fred pointed. "Get back here or I'll kill you with—!"

Leo shifted into drive and floored the pedal. Dust and gravel showered the Jeep as Leo shot uphill.

In the rearview mirror, Fred punched the air before disappearing in the gray cloud. Leo glided around a U-turn and sped up the next ascent. Below, the Jeep emerged, hunting him. Sweating all over, Leo lunged through a slack S-turn and got ready to drift around another bend.

Fred couldn't catch him, but what if he reported him? That would be the end of his adventures. The Polaris had the upper hand while climbing the canyon, but once Leo reached the plateau, he could only press his off-roader to eighty miles per hour.

While tackling the second to last U-bend, the desert landscape of the Valley of the Gods rushed past, adorned with green shrubs, orange buttes, and rock towers. Far below, the Jeep crawled around a turn.

As Leo hurried along the rocky wall, he maneuvered the Polaris like an extension of himself, anticipating every bump like a seasoned equestrian predicts his horse's strides. His mind processed millions of calculations as he followed the optimal racing line, cutting corners with millimeter precision—man and machine, one.

Adrenaline rushed through his veins as Leo danced around the last bend and the transmission belt responded as if synced with his nervous system. The terror of Fred catching him drowned in the sheer excitement of the runaway. It was wrong, but he couldn't help it. If nothing else, *this* Leo mastered. Blasting through the rocky desert like a jet fighter skimming the ground left an unmatched smile on his face.

He was sure Fred was snailing around down there somewhere. "God, make his engine boil. Amen."

Clear skies opened as he reached the top. The cracked asphalt stretched into the endless upland of the Cedar Mesa, and bushes and sandy rocky fields extended to the horizon.

Every string of his body loosened. "Freedom!" Leo hollered and burst into laughter. His only joy. The racing gloves creaked as he released the grip on the wheel, fingers aching.

The headset rang. "Bro'," Leo said. "I'll call you back—"

"Leo, this is Mom. Are you all right?"

"Oh, hi . . ."

"Answer me. You okay?!"

"I'm fine! Just slid on the gravel, that's all."

"You better be careful."

"I'm not an amateur, you know." The silence stabbed, bleeding out his happiness. Why did she have to kill his only escape? If there was anyone who gave him a beating for his past, it was himself.

"I want you to stay home tonight."

He hit the steering wheel. "You kiddin' me?! Mom! Tomorrow's Monday. Why can't I have some light in my life?"

"Light? What does that mean? What are you doing on that ranch, anyway?"

"I'm twenty soon, Mom. Can't I have my own life?"

His mother sighed. "You know I love you, right?"

"Yes—way too much. And that's the problem."

"You're so cute when you're angry. Did you know that?"

Leo rolled his eyes. "I'm hanging up, Mom. See you at supper."

Headlights bounced in the mirrors. Fred had gained on him, and Leo had to hide in the terrain. Had the man seen his license plate?

Leo turned left onto a sandy and bouncy trail for half a mile and made another left. The path led him back toward the twisting descent into the Valley, eventually taking him home across the Arizona border.

Low vegetation swooshed past on both sides and dust whirled in the rear—no sign of the Jeep. Despite deep grooves and bumps, Leo maintained thirty miles per hour.

Far past the road down the canyon, he entered a trail leading back to the paved road. His body felt familiarly beaten from absorbing the impacts. As he drew near the road, he scouted for the Jeep. All clear—almost too good to be true. He entered and sighed, knowing behind the next bend began the descent of Moki Dugway.

Tires squealed as the Jeep emerged, charging from the opposite direction with a tail of blue smoke. Leo stamped the brake, threw the steering around, and mashed the throttle. Fred flashed the auxiliary lights and honked. What if he had crashed into a crazy person? Maybe Fred really wanted to kill him?

But this was Leo's backyard. Problem was, south of the dugway was the dead end of Cedar Mesa. Nothing but drops all around. Leo flew off the asphalt onto another path, bouncing as he hurried over holes and humps.

Suddenly, the ground disappeared and his wheels spun midair. The landing knocked the breath out of him. Gasping, he steered frantically, trying to get his bearings. He slowed down, groaning from pain in his back. *Oh, no.* The oil lamp lit and the engine temperature was rising. He had to pull over soon before the engine got damaged.

Leo veered off the sandy trail and drove toward a rock formation, flattening bushes. He pulled around a boulder and parked only two hundred feet from a ravine.

He stepped out and pulled off his helmet. Coarse black locks whipped against his neck, soaked. His tanned skin glinted in the burning sun, and he unzipped the chest of his white racing suit. Blue and silver lines ran from shoulder to leg. Fiddling with his goatee, he noticed a black bird encircling him—if only he had wings . . .

A low rumble froze his heart. He moved past the steaming Polaris and peeked around the boulder. The Jeep was creeping toward him, bouncing over rocks, following his trail. The man smelled blood. Fred *was* going to kill him.

He opened the glove box and stuffed the insurance slip and wallet in one pocket, and the keys, his smartphone, and a New Testament Bible in another. Could anything lead back to him except the license plate?

Crawling around in his off-roader, Leo searched for his tools but got out and slammed the door. They were lying at the bottom of the dugway with his climbing equipment.

Leo hid his gloves and helmet in a bush while scanning the ground for a sharp stone that would fit the screws on his plate. The Jeep's engine growled like a bear in the distance. Finally, he spotted a flat stone and sprinted around his vehicle.

He fumbled. A close fit. "Come on! Stupid rock!" Leo flung the stone as his pocket vibrated. He grabbed his phone. Butterflies fluttered in his stomach. *Incoming Call. Probation Officer C. Archer.*

"Why now?!" Leo hissed. "There's no check-ins till tomorrow!" The Jeep honked angrily, startling him. "God." Leo fought back tears, ignoring the call. "Give me an excuse he'll buy." The phone stopped vibrating.

The Jeep rumbled louder. He seized the license plate and pulled. It snapped and he flung onto his back, sand showering his sticky skin. The bird above croaked and dove behind a rocky ridge. Leo stumbled to his feet, hoping Fred's anger would blind him from finding the chassis number—he didn't dare think about his probation officer getting wind of this.

Leo ran along the rocky wall and crouched behind a stone close to the mesa's edge. Trapped, but hidden. The black bird landed on the boulder that concealed his precious Polaris. He stared at his license plate, then at the rocky ridge next to him, and tossed. The plate landed somewhere on the top, out of sight.

Beyond the plateau's edge stretched the twisting gorge carved by the San Juan River. Far in the distance stood Monument Valley's red-rock buttes—pillars preventing the sky from crushing the earth, he used to believe. His home lay in the shelter of what looked like a sharp tooth. How he wished he could run up to his room and hide!

Sweat seared his eye. He rubbed his face in the crook of his elbow, feeling the scar on his forehead. The humming stopped, and he curled himself tightly, resting his back against the stone, a deadly drop only thirty feet away.

Voices shouted in conversation, and he peeked out. Fred's orange mustache gleamed above wide shoulders wrapped in a muscle shirt as he trampled around the boulder. "I know you're here, punk!"

Leo pressed himself against the hot stone, embracing his knees, trembling.

"Come out and don't embarrass yourself! You hit the wrong guy!"

He heard something thumped his vehicle and the fear vaporized. Leo clenched his fists.

"C'mon and face me like a man!" Fred roared.

His heart pumped a little courage around his system. What if he sprinted with all his might? Maybe he could get around him? But his Polaris would only survive a mile or two . . . what about hijacking the Jeep? Did Fred leave the keys in? But what about the old man in the passenger seat . . . yes, that was his best chance—pleading with the oldster to tame this beast.

"Irresponsible coward!" Twigs snapped under heavy boots. "I'm a specialized accident attorney, you know. You like to know what thoughts I think grind you mad right now? I know everything about *accidents*."

Fred grunted, and a stone bulleted past Leo off the cliff. "Divine justice has hunted you down."

"Fred!" a distant voice shouted. "Git back here. Let the young'un be!"

"Soon finished, Papa!" The trampling drew nearer. "Where are you?" Fred whispered.

His shadow appeared. Leo held his breath, ready for the sprint of his life.

Leather boots and tree trunk legs jumped in front of him, blocking him. Leo gaped at the tattooed man flexing his arms and shaking his head. "What a spectacle." The man grabbed Leo's suit and lifted him off the ground.

"No!" Leo wriggled. "Let me go!"

Fred nudged Leo's tufted beard and laughed. "Only men with confidence grow a goatee."

"Let me down or I'll report you!"

"And what do you think I'll do?"

"Fred, son!" the old man said from a distance. "Don't skeer the fella!"

He pulled Leo up close to his face, his breath reeking of garlic. "Tomorrow, I'm reporting you to the police, but I want—"

"Please don't! What can I do to—"

"Shut it! I want to teach you a lesson, son. You must think I'm crazy—and I hope I've scared you silly—but let's just say I'm passionate. I see way too many kids at your age destroying themselves with everything from social media to drugs. This is your wake-up call—one you'll never forget. If you'd stepped out of your toy back there, we would have done all the paperwork and be eating dinner with our mommas right now. Promise me one thing, and I'll let you down. Tomorrow I will report the accident, but it seems like I've already forgotten about the race I've enjoyed."

"No! Don't go to the police. Can I pay you here and—"

"I don't want your money—I want your future secured. Swear on your little life or I'll report the entire story, including my video of you racing up the hills like some headless chicken." Fred tightened his grip. "Agree?"

Leo swallowed and nodded.

"Vow you'll stay away from drugs, take care of your family, and that you never flee from your responsibilities again. Be a man, for heaven's sake!" Leo closed his eyes and clenched his teeth. "You hear me?!" Leo nodded. "Promise me!"

"I p-promise," Leo whimpered. "I swear!"

The man pressed a business card into Leo's pocket and dropped him. Leo collapsed to the ground.

Fred took a few steps and turned. "Looking forward to meeting you as a trustworthy man one day, kiddo." The man walked away.

Leo squeezed his fingers into the soil, sobbing. He had thought Fred would throw him off the cliff—that would have been better. Then there'd be no more problems. What should he say when his probation officer finds out? Maybe he should run away and start a new life? But where? And how?

Fred disappeared past the Polaris, and Leo dried his nose, stumbled to his feet, and pulled up the business card. *Fred Waylon. If you struggle with the old, you're a fighter toward the new. Get a free counseling session by answering the following question—*Leo shredded the card.

What should he do? He would destroy his vehicle if he drove it, and he certainly wouldn't ask Fred for a ride. Could there be any houses around? Leo looked up at the rocky hedge leading up to his off-roader. The license plate . . .

The Jeep fired up and drove off as Leo climbed the ridge. Gingerly, he clambered over the top. The other side curved into a crack, and a creek gurgled below. Luckily, his license plate stuck to the curving side, close to an empty bird's nest. Leo shaded his eyes. Not a single rooftop or shed anywhere.

He knelt and bent forward to grab the license plate when something flapped into Leo's side, startling him off balance.

"Help!" Leo gasped as he fell on his stomach, headfirst, grasping the sandstone. His weight pulled him relentlessly down the slippery side. "Help me!" A bird cawed around him as his fingers grasped a crack, causing his legs to slip down and leaving him hanging.

"Anyone!" The hand was losing grip. "Fred! Help me!" His fingers slipped. "My God!" Leo squealed, grasping at every passing rock, root, and crack. All snapped out of his hands. *I'm gonna die, I'm gonna die.* "God, help me!"

Chapter 2

WOUNDED

Could death embrace Leo so softly or had he plunged into mud? He opened his eyes. A bright ray pierced through blurry cascades of sandstone. Leo inhaled and sharp pain stung his side. He gritted his teeth and groaned, breathing slowly. Some thirty feet above, between undulating walls of a bending crevice, snaked the blue sky. A long drizzle of sand ended just above his head. A single beam of sunlight passed the stone walls, warming his legs.

Carefully, he sat up in a dune like the silkiest of beaches. His tongue stuck to his mouth and his throat burned. *Water* . . . He swallowed what felt like shards of glass, tasting blood. Leo sneezed and tears popped. "*Ahh!*" He touched his side and moaned.

The sandy floor meandered between walls ornamentally carved by wind and flash floods. An eerie whistle blew through the ravine, which was deep-purple at the bottom, brown in the middle, and bright yellow at the top. The freedom he so enjoyed felt as unreachable as the crack of blue above.

Gingerly, Leo rose to his feet and pulled out his smartphone. He swiped the cracked black screen, shaking his head. Leo had broken his ribs before, but never in an abandoned place like this. Laboriously swallowing, he gazed up, recalling the sound of a brook.

A clucking from behind startled him. "Kiddo," a hoarse voice said. A raven stood on a sculptured ledge, cocking its head. "Kiddo," the bird mimicked. "Kiii-do. Ki-do-do."

He launched his phone at the bird and it shattered on the shelf. "Feathered beast!" Leo doubled over and covered his ribs, whimpering.

The bird flapped above his head and disappeared into the crevice.

"Speaking bird . . . a demon," Leo said between gritted teeth. He fought tears and focused on calming his breathing. What had happened remained between him and that raven. No one could ever know that a birdie had overcome him—and definitely not his brother.

Leo shuffled tiny steps and supported himself against the cold sandstone. As the walls increasingly glowed orange, water gurgled louder in the singing breeze.

He stalled and dropped his jaw. Before a naturally formed arch lay a wooden bucket tied to a rope. Could it be? Did climbers rappel down here to get spring water? Should he wait for somebody to come? What if a climber had just been here? Leo's pulse raced. "Help me!" he shouted, and immediately regretted it at the jab of grinding bones. He focused on calming his breathing again, dried his cheeks, and limped toward the bucket.

Green water funneled through a neighboring ravine twenty feet below and disappeared into a dark cave. Lightheaded, Leo knelt and grabbed the container. With the rope already tied to a heavy stone, he lowered it into the fast-flowing stream. The current filled the bucket but snapped the rope out of his hands.

Leo sighed, staring at the rope and the heavily bouncing container—it was too painful to pull. "Great. Now what?" After rock climbing all day, and dodging Fred, he was parched. Who knew when he'd find water again?

Wincing, he wrapped the rope around his boot and hobbled away, dragging it with his heel, and as the bucket finally came over the edge, it tipped. "No!" He lunged. A sip left, full of sand.

Leo dropped the bucket into the creek. The irresistibly clear water pulled the rope tight—even the trickling sounded brisk. He fell to the ground, this time crawling backwards, slowly pulling the rope with his foot, moaning. The top of the bucket appeared, and he walked on the rope to grab it.

"Gotcha." He gulped it half empty, spilling spring water down his outfit. How could water taste so good, refreshing even his mind?! Leo returned everything to the way he found it and spotted footprints leading farther into the crevice. "Thank God, a way out."

As he inched along, the ravine descended deeper into the earth. *At least it's cool down here.* Leo followed the footmarks through several widened openings where beams of sunlight hit the sand, coloring the stonewalls like massive embers, towering a hundred feet tall. He paused in each ray to feel the sun on his face and say a brief prayer:

"God, I believe in You."

"I know You are real and good. Help me out of here."

"Do You only help good people, God? How about bad ones?"

"I know I'm not a good person. Can you still help me, God? Amen?"

"Our Father in heaven, hallowed be Your name. Your kingdom come. Your . . . Your . . . ? For Yours is the kingdom and the power and the glory forever. Amen."

"Okay. It wasn't good to run away from the accident. I'll admit that." Leo squinted at the sky and sighed. His leg muscles ached from catching his steps in the descending crevice. "Can you forgive me? Just want to get home before—"

"Kiddo," the guttural voice said, echoing from behind the next turn.

Quietly, Leo left the sunray and headed toward the bend. "Kiii-do-do."

Leo grabbed a pebble and lurked along the sandstone. Sliding his fingers in the grooves, he peeked around the corner. He gaped. Behind the light-pillar of the widest space yet, stood an old cabin. A twisting juniper tree grew up one wall, along the roof, and its ancient crown canopied a reddish tin roof, slightly deforming the building. The roots stood raised above the sand, and chopped wood lay next to the trunk.

The raven landed on a branch and flapped its wings. "Kiddo."

The stone slid out of his hand as Leo approached the meager cabin. Neither its door nor single window fit their frames. Through one of the weathered wooden walls, turned silver with age, jutted a chimney that was bent to avoid smoking the green, scale-like leaves.

Leo stopped halfway toward the next sunbeam. "Hello?! Anybody there?!"

The raven cawed, swooped past him, and disappeared around a corner. He followed and stared into an arid side-canyon ending alongside a river miles away. Leo shaded his eyes as he stepped through the crevice opening. *That's San Juan River, but ... where am I?*

A narrow pathway secured only by a frayed rope led from the opening down to the river. His fractured ribs made the trail's obstacles—rocks and sharp bends—torturous. He had to call 911. Maybe they could get him a helicopter? But more importantly, he had to call his mother. She would expect him soon, and if he didn't reach her to sugarcoat his delay—or she didn't get to him—she would call the police before the evening was over.

Leo withdrew and trudged toward the hut. "Anybody home?!" He groaned, holding his tender rib. The injury felt swollen.

Dust danced around the sun's spotlight, and the overgrowing age-old juniper made it clear that whoever lived here was not in a hurry. Did this person even know what a phone was?

He knocked. Only the cool mountain breeze rustled in the branches. Could the owner be sleeping? Leo knocked harder and the door squeaked open. "Hello? Anyone there?" Sweet incense wafted out from the lonely dwelling.

Instead of a spider-infested scene from a scary movie, the home felt welcoming as he trod onto the creaky floor. A lantern illumined a wooden table with two low stools. Embers glowed in the ash of a freestanding fireplace and an iron pot sat on top. On a small kitchen bench stood bowls of olives and dried dates, a honey jar, and pots with fresh herbs. Cupboards, bookshelves, and a thick rug lay on the floor. No bed or mattresses anywhere.

Below the only window was a prayer bench before a low table covered with half-burned candles, small icons, dozens of tiny vials of water, and an incense holder emitting thin curling smoke. A few papyrus scrolls and a pile of old books stood on a long shelf. On the wall hung an icon of Jesus Christ wearing a dark robe, holding a book, and the left side of His face appeared different from His right.

Light from the crevice opening shone through the window onto an antique book on a bookstand. He moved up close and turned the stiff pages of what looked like Hebrew. Many pages seemed like they had been out in the rain at some point.

"Glad you feel at home, little prophet," a man's voice said.

Leo jumped and turned too fast. "I'm sorry! I didn't—it was open . . . I haven't taken—*ahh!*" He shielded his side with a shaking hand.

A thin man in sandals stepped toward him, wearing worn pants and a dark-green cloak tied with a leather belt. Untrimmed locks of brown hair and beard covered his chest and shoulders. Fiery golden-brown eyes gleamed beneath knitted brows on his tanned face. He looked raggedy yet youthful, modest but captivating. Slowly, he reached his hand toward Leo's side. "Let me see."

Leo stepped back. "Don't come near me! Who are you?"

"I know you're wounded."

"Let me out! I haven't stolen anything."

The man raised his arms disarmingly. "Why would I think you're a thief? Let me take a look."

"You're a witch doctor or something?"

The stranger crossed himself, shaking his head. "I won't hurt you."

"Then promise you won't touch."

His fiery eyes seemed to dance with joy as he looked at Leo. "Able to unzip and get your shoulder out of that suit?"

"I want a sedative before you do anything."

The man smiled. "I'm not a doctor, but a close Friend of mine is."

Leo raised his eyebrows. "Then don't come near me."

"I said I won't touch you. I know I may look scary, but I'd be most honored to help you."

Leo snorted. "You would?" He studied the stranger. *If this is the closest to the ER out here, then* . . . Leo sighed, unzipped slowly, and groaned as he pushed out his shoulder. He rolled up his t-shirt, unveiling red and purple swellings.

The man opened his palms. "Okay, Leo. I won't touch you, but can you take my hands?"

Leo shot him a startled glance. "Hey, I didn't tell you my name—no."

The long-haired man smiled. "Trust me. God loves you."

Leo was taken aback. Gently, he took hold of the man's hands.

The owner lifted his face and closed his eyes. "Our dear Lord. We, Your feeble creatures, yet so loved, come to find grace in a time of need. Your son has three broken ribs and two fractures. But Your blood heals."

Heat flowed from the praying man's hands, circling Leo's arms, and reached his shoulders, strangely ticklish. His mind told him to let go, but he couldn't—didn't want to. The invisible currents flowed around Leo's ribcage and he inhaled, unsure whether to laugh or scream. Leo twitched at the sound of popping and his ribs stopped throbbing.

"Thank you, Lord, for placing Your hands on my brother's wound." Tears ran from the recluse's closed eyes.

Leo's ribcage seemed to absorb the swirling rivers of warmth and the stinging pain faded.

"Thank you, Almighty Lord, for answering the prayer of your smallest of servants. We will always worship you. Forever and ever. Amen." The man opened clear eyes and chuckled, apparently because of Leo's face expression.

Slowly, Leo looked under his arm. The bruises had vanished. Gently, he touched his side. No pain. "What did you just do?!"

The man laughed. "Didn't you see? I talked with your Healer."

Leo bent, twisted, and turned. "Man, that was . . . you're good at this. Never thought prayer could work like that . . ." Outside the window, a gust of wind entered the crevice and whipped up sand. "So . . . do you have a phone as well? And if not, can God answer a prayer for, you know . . ."

"Don't you want to thank God for what He just did?"

Leo rubbed his neck. "Yeah, I should. Can't believe what just happened."

"Now is a good time to start."

"How did you know my name? And how did you count the fractures?"

The hermit beamed. "I'm the Lord's most unworthy servant. I've been waiting for you, Leo."

He shrunk back. "But I don't know you . . . and you've been stalking me. How do I know you're not the second crazy person I've met today?"

"How can I prove to you I'm a friend who loves God?"

"Well . . ." Leo zipped his racing suit. "Point taken."

"Don't you also love the Lord, Leo?"

"So, I've only been a Christian for almost three months. Pretty new to it all."

"You'll learn quickly." The recluse reached out his hand. "Call me Johnny."

Leo greeted him—an unexpectedly soft handshake for his bony figure. To Leo's amazement, the man didn't reek of sweat, but smelled like a flowery meadow.

"I know millions of questions are running through your mind right now. But do you drink tea?"

"I'm kinda in a hurry."

Johnny nodded toward a stool. "I handmade that seat long ago. It's been empty ever since."

Leo didn't know if this was creepy or amazing, but with the agonizing injury gone, he owed the man some courtesy. He had heard about healing, and read a few stories in the Gospels, but that God would heal him like this? Beyond belief.

"But you aren't fully healed yet, little prophet." Johnny finished putting herbs and honey in the pot.

"What?"

He put the kettle on the fireplace and lit the wood. "I prepared this for you earlier today." Johnny put the bowls with dried fruits on the table and sat across from him.

Leo leaned back. "You waited for me? How? This is disturbing, you know."

The bearded man nodded. "The Kingdom of God is a completely new world for you to discover. Once you befriend the Ruler of the Universe, everything changes."

Was Johnny trying to recruit him into some weird sect?

Johnny laughed. "Your call differs from mine, little prophet. Don't fear I'm trying to manipulate you."

"Hey!" Leo rose and stepped backward. "Stop doing that. Get out of my head."

Johnny moved and stirred the tea. "Forgive me. Like I told you. I'm one of the Lord's most useless servants. I'm trying to connect with you."

"Don't try so hard or you'll scare me, okay?"

The solitary took his seat and opened his palms. "Let's give thanks for this meal."

Leo returned to his seat.

Johnny seemed focused, eyes closed. "Go ahead, you pray, Leo."

"Uh . . . dear God. Thank you for this food—and for the tea. Amen."

"In Jesus' name I pray. Amen," Johnny added.

Leo's stomach growled and he blushed, and Johnny handed him both bowls.

"Eat as much as you can, little prophet. Long day ahead of you."

He ate some of the sweetest dates he'd ever tasted that melted on his tongue. "So, God told you about me? That's how you know everything?"

Johnny grinned, his light-brown eyes blazing. "He gives Himself freely and completely to us, and He allows us to keep Him—our treasure in earthen vessels—even though He's fully sovereign. His life is ours when we're fully His."

"Mm-hm. Would it be possible to borrow your phone?"

"Something urgent?"

"Don't you already know?"

"You told me to stay out of your head . . ."

"You know, I didn't plan to fall into your backyard. Need to let Mom know I'm well."

"You think she'll call the police?"

"I do."

"That a problem?"

"Of course it is. It's completely unnecessary."

Johnny got the whistling teapot and filled two wooden bowls. "What happens if she does?"

Leo crossed his arms. Does Johnny know he'll lose his driver's license or not?

"Johnny," a throaty voice said outside the door. "Jo-Jo-Johnny."

"Oh, Bikki." Johnny leaned toward the door and opened. The black raven, holding a cookie, jumped onto the kitchen bench. "Thank you, my friend."

Leo pointed. "It's that beast! It's his fault I fell down here."

"It's just a bird, Leo." Johnny held the door open and the raven flew outside. "Bikki is God's gift to me."

"Seriously?! That creature knocked me off balance, so I . . ."

Johnny closed the door. "Can you forgive him?"

Leo shook his head. "Yeah, whatever."

"During all these years out here, Bikki has brought me a cookie each day. Don't ask me where he gets them. But never, ever has he brought me a young man . . ."

"What does that mean?"

"Means you're chosen, Leo."

Leo searched for any sign of technology. "You don't have a phone, do you, Johnny?"

"Don't need any."

"Well, I'm pretty squeezed right now 'cause I need to get home before Mom calls the cops." Leo rose. "Thank you for the prayer and the hospitality."

"Afraid that your freedom adventures will end?"

Leo raised his eyebrows and headed for the door. "Thank you for healing my ribs. Goodbye."

"Don't leave me, little prophet. Not yet."

THE LEGEND OF THE DIVINE CALENDAR

He stepped outside. "I don't have a choice. But I'll come back with a gift or something—I'll ask Mom if I can swap my weekend duties and come next Saturday. Promise. I want to become a better Christian and believe harder and pray longer. Clearly, I know nothing of what I've prayed myself into."

"Don't do this, Leo. I beg you."

Leo waved. "Sorry, Johnny. I won't forget where to find you." He jogged toward the crevice opening and something darted past him. "One more time, Bikki . . ." The raven circled around the beam of sunshine.

"Little prophet!" Johnny stepped outside. "Trust me when I say your freedom adventures are not your only source of joy."

Leo stopped and pointed. "You know nothing about that, Johnny! If the police find out about this day, they'll revoke my license and my only means of getting fresh air." He stretched out his arms. "I just want to be me, totally free. Nothing wrong with that."

The hermit dropped to his knees in the sand, hands folded. "Please, Leo. Trust God when I tell you that even though He just healed your body, you're still bleeding."

Leo stepped backwards, waving his hand. "Hey, get up! Don't kneel like that."

"Stay for the afternoon. I'll get you home before it's too late."

"You don't know my mom." He stepped into the sunlight seeping from the mouth of the crevice. "By the way, how would you get me home?"

Johnny, still on his knees, pointed up.

Leo sighed. "I can't. I don't have your faith. See you, Johnny." He turned and jogged through the opening.

"I was there, Leo!" Johnny's voice echoed.

Still running, he glanced over his shoulder. "Where?!"

"In Parker. I watched the race."

It felt like the words shattered something deep within and he skidded to a halt. "What race!?"

Johnny stumbled to his feet. "I was in the crowd. Cheering you on."

Leo felt nauseous. "Impossible! Don't lie to me, Johnny."

"I would never. I was there when you couldn't afford the car."

Leo could hear his heartbeat. His right hand trembled. "That can't be true."

The man held his hands to his chest. "And I was there on January 24th."

"No!" Leo roared and darted toward him. The world spun but his feet kept running, locking in on the wild man as his target, who seemingly braced for impact. "You were not!" He slammed into Johnny, who stumbled backwards. "Leave me alone!" Leo fell onto his knees, shrieking and hammering the man's thighs. "You had no right to be there!" His voice cracked as his energy leaked into the sand. "Get away from me," Leo hissed, his throat sore.

"It's okay, little prophet." Johnny wept and knelt, and Leo felt his embrace.

"No-no. It's never gonna be okay." He whispered. Leo collapsed into Johnny's shoulder. Darkness enclosed him. But Leo knew he could not leave this man.

Chapter 3

THE DIVINE CALENDAR

Leo's hands ached and throat burned as he peeked from the corner where he sat wrapped in a blanket. The sunset glowed in the cabin's only window. With his cloaked back toward Leo, the man of God knelt before his overfilled prayer altar, and sunbeams projected his scruffy outline across the room.

Johnny exhaled quietly, shoulders shuddering. "My heart breaks for him, Lord," the hermit whispered. "I see what You've shown me—but how? He's so young."

Sweet incense curled from the low table, and some fifty candles flickered with pocket-sized icons before them. Leo wanted to ask Johnny to implore God to change Fred's mind about reporting his escape from the accident.

The prayerful man lifted his face. "How magnificent, how beautiful You are, my Lord and Bridegroom. And how unqualified I am to be Your friend. I bring my son, Leo, before Your merciful eyes."

My son? What does he want from me?
"My Lord, embrace Leo's soul."
Peace like an invisible blanket descended on him, and Leo lowered his shoulders and exhaled, his pulse relaxing.
His host dried his face with his sleeve. "Grant him peace. Can You awaken him?"
The sore side of Leo's hands throbbed. Oh, the man's poor legs . . . Leo had treated him like a punching bag. Why did God allow Johnny to see what no one should probe into? Shouldn't God respect his privacy?
Johnny arose and Leo closed his eyes. Wood creaked across the cabin and Johnny poured something. Leo swallowed, breathing in a sleeping pace. The floorboards squeaked and the smell of mint leaves wafted.
"I've let it cool for some minutes, little prophet. It'll be perfect for your throat."
Johnny's tender voice broke Leo's act. The solitary crouched, smiling, mostly with his eyes. Leo blinked at his bright countenance. Even though Johnny had an alfresco appearance, he wasn't dirty. Rather, Leo felt dirty in his presence.
"I don't deserve your never-ending care," Leo whispered hoarsely. The mint tea, rich with honey, soothed his voice.
Johnny received Leo's empty tea bowl. "Forgive me. I had no choice."
"Forgive you?! Aren't your legs hurting?"
"My heart is. I felt your pain."
Leo straightened his back against the wall. "Sorry about all that. Kinda lost it for a moment."
"Glad you found it again." Leo cocked his head, and Johnny reached his hand and pulled him up. "Ready to talk?"
"Will you help me get home?"

"Still worried about that? Yes, God is in control."

Leo rubbed his neck—everything felt out of control. "Like I said, I prayed my first prayer to Jesus and bought this New Testament." He patted his bulging pocket. "Read a chapter each day, and three months later—voilà. My faith is still nothing compared to yours."

"Don't say that. Remember the mustard seed?"

"Mustard seed?"

Johnny smiled and nodded. "Okay, want to take a seat?"

Leo got up on the simple stool. Wood crackled in the fireplace, and Leo unzipped the top of his racing suit.

The hermit put dried fruit on the table and sat across from him. "Volkswagen Polo R WRC? You must tell me about that at some point."

Leo stared. Was Johnny's tanned skin shining or just reflecting the lantern on the table? "I followed your footsteps but saw no signs of you. How did you suddenly know I was in your home?"

"Bikki alerted me, so I hurried back from my daily shopping."

"Shopping?"

"Didn't you notice the beehives on your way?"

Leo shook his head. "I know this area, but heard no rumors about you. Are you a Navajo?"

"Oh, I'm not from here, and I travel at night. Lived in these parts for sixteen years."

"Sixteen?! How old are you?"

"Oh, time out here means little. The earth keeps spinning and seasons come and go, nothing escaping the commands of the Lord. That's my grasp of time. I follow the heavenly calendar."

"I used to let the stars speak to me as well. So, what are you, forty?"

Johnny scratched his beard. "Somewhere around there . . . I've been waiting here for the Chosen Steward."

"The who?"

Johnny looked him deeply in the eyes. "The one I can entrust with my mystery."

Oh, no . . . Just because Johnny's guard bird attacked him, pushing him down here, didn't mean he was called to this wild man's fantasies. Besides, as his clash with Fred emphasized, he was anything but responsible. Leo helped his mom pay the bills, but his trustworthiness ended there. "Why do you live like this? Do you have a family somewhere?"

The recluse leaned back and folded his hands, exhaling. "My parents' faith meant everything to them. They loved God intensely, breathing prayers, so they consecrated me to God before I was born. Therefore, I also wanted to serve God with all my being. Always felt God's holy fire in my heart."

"Are you a monk?"

Johnny's eyes flared intimidatingly, but his warm presence kept Leo on his stool. "My parents led me to a community who lived an austere life in the countryside. After a few years with them, still a young teenager, I moved into the wild and lived alone in prayer night and day."

"Skipped school and all that?!"

"Wouldn't say that. I'm still the Lord's student. The ascetic community taught me to read and write, and to survive from what nature provided. Our Heavenly Father taught me what I needed to know. God's Spirit subdued the earth before me and I befriended the animals."

"Seriously?!"

Johnny laughed and nodded.

"Man, I'm really sorry about my attitude toward Bikki. I'll behave. But why move here?"

"Over the years, the Lord taught me more than a human heart can contain. Now I have one burden left on my heart. Frankly, it's the reason the Lord directed me out here."

"What's your burden?" Leo blurted. *Stupid, Leo. Stupid. Don't dig into this.*

"Oh, should I just reveal my treasure that easily?"

"No, you shouldn't."

"Okay. Little prophet. If you answer a few of my questions, I'll tell you what my burden is. Deal?"

It was probably a mistake, but Leo agreed. He had to admit he was curious.

"Why is your mother so concerned about you?"

"Because she's expecting me by now."

"Why?"

Leo kept rotating the bowl with dried figs. "Mom carried the responsibility for my brother and me. My father left us when I was little—no memory of him. Mom is a real heroine. It wasn't easy for her to raise us, being foreign to the Navajos and all. Now I know how tough it was for her with full-time work, taking care of us, living among the Navajo culture, and dealing with our kind but snoopy neighbors."

"What's her name?"

"Angelina Avens. She's American, but lived in Italy until we moved to Arizona when I was two."

"Why settle among the natives?"

"Long story. Mom wishes she could change one thing about me, though."

"Which is?"

"Does that count as a question?"

"You're a bit too clever, Leo. We need to polish that."

"She wishes I would trade my Polaris and climbing gear for reading glasses and a chessboard."

Johnny chuckled. "Can't blame her. Actually, she wishes you would trade your need for adrenaline with accepting your probation, and your need for accomplishments with believing you're worthy of love."

Leo's smile shrunk. The words sliced him—but, as if soaked with oil, they immediately treated the pain.

The man's steady gaze seemed to corner him. "There's a recent scar on your forehead and you're not at peace. What are you running from?"

Leo sat up straight and sniffed. "Nothing. Just love spending my spare time riding in the desert, camping, and climbing." He was sure the man looked into his soul.

"That's your only joy because it's your private world. Little prophet, why is your heart closed up? Even to God?"

"If it is, it's for protection."

The dim reflection of a different sun shone on the man across the table. "It's because your heart is acutely wounded. Leo, you're bleeding. You run away to protect yourself."

Leo wiped his nose. "There's nothing I can do about that."

"Oh, it is. But I can't take that pain away from you. Only One can." Johnny touched his shoulder. "But you think God can never forgive you. That He can never heal you."

Even if Johnny was right, Leo wouldn't admit it. This was none of his business. How could Johnny's words keep invading his thoughts? And with such force? He didn't need healing, did he? Forgiveness, oh absolutely—as a newbie Christian, he knew

God had forgiven his mistakes, even though he struggled with accepting it. But healing? . . .

Johnny's light-brown eyes pierced him again. "The wound in your soul bleeds every time you encounter someone who knows what happened."

"But what if I don't want the pain to go away? What if I deserve it? I see it on all those faces every night before I fall asleep. They stare at me. Anger. Disgust. Disappointment—smeared all over them. What if they're right?!"

"But if you're honest, you want to be healed—even though you may think it's only suppressed memories—because this wound is slowly killing you." Leo's chin quavered. "Last question," Johnny continued, "and I'll tell you why you're here. What happened on January 24th?"

Leo stared into his palms. "Can't tell you, because . . ." He lifted his face. "I'm not ready to talk to anyone living about it."

The man of God sat silent with knitted brows.

Don't you dare come near . . .

Johnny went to the prayer corner, the unbearable light moving off Leo, and returned with a notebook and a papyrus scroll sealed with red wax. "The Kingdom of God is full of concealed mysteries unknown even to the angels. And the Holy Spirit unveils these mysteries at specific times to realign the flow of history."

"The flow of history? Realign toward what?"

The cabin creaked and the sunshine flickered. Outside, a little whirlwind glided toward them and sand entered the cracks, leaving yellow strands on the floor.

Johnny slid the notebook toward Leo, engraved with a clamshell holding a pearl. "Forgive me for pushing you, little prophet. You've earned the right to receive my treasure now."

Leo opened the book and the binding creaked. "What am I doing?"

The hermit gave him a pen. "You will not understand much of what I'm about to tell you, but years from now, you'll guard this notebook like gold. I know you're not the journaling type, but remember, God already healed your fractured bones. He seeks your attention."

Leo swallowed and put the pen to the yellowed paper. "All right. I'll do my best."

"Imagine time is like a train traveling through many stations before reaching its final destination. Each stop allows more passengers to board, and the train stations represent events in history when God's purposes reach fulfillment."

Leo looked up from the journal. "What do you mean?"

"Fulfillment of prophecies. The stations are events God has already announced will impact humanity to lead travelers onto His train. But unknown to the passengers, undercover bandits try to hijack and derail the train, pushing time out of its appointed track. The bandits want to rewrite prophecy. However, among the passengers are a chosen few who understand what the robbers try to accomplish. These chosen men and women counteract the bandits and realign the train toward its next station so more passengers can board. The chosen want to fulfill prophecy.

"There's a battle over the train of time between those who seek to derail and realign its course. And when evil has diverted it, God calls on His chosen to redirect the flow of history."

Leo glanced at Johnny, and the teacher paused. "Okay . . ." Leo said as he finished writing. "What does this have to do with me?"

"Many years ago, God unlocked for me a mystery that put the events of everyone's life in reference to one Man. The Proto-Man. The life of the Proto-Man repeats again and again in every person's life. If you understand the Proto-Man's life—the Proto-Life—you'll understand what is happening in your life. Imagine if Someone had lived your life before you. Wouldn't you like to know this Life, to better understand your own?"

Leo cracked his fingers and shook sand off his boots. "Sounds amazing—and way above my paygrade."

"I know, and that's why you're taking excellent notes so you can receive true wealth one day." Leo tilted his head. "What I'm saying, Leo, is that this mystery can not only heal your inner wound, but show you how it can serve the purpose of your life."

Leo's pulse increased and he narrowed his eyes, shoulders tense. But when Johnny closed his eyes, Leo relaxed. "Do you mean . . . I can think like God?"

"You won't take His place, but you can understand His ways with you."

"I can understand God?"

Johnny touched the scroll on the table. "Would you like to? Little prophet?"

The few Christians Leo knew talked about knowing God all the time, but he had never thought about it like this. Could he change his past?

"God is still God, and He is mighty to work all things together for good to those who love Him. But for God's will to be fulfilled in our phase of history, many human souls must be healed and released into their God-given purpose. They must board the train of God's history. Only then will God move the world closer to the last station of this age."

Leo turned a page, wrote as fast as he could, and looked up. Johnny smiled, and Leo scratched his neck. "So, the Proto-Man is the first man, right? Adam?"

The hermit shook his head. "The Proto-Man is Jesus Christ. You see, this mystery I will explain to you will restore key souls, but it's been hidden since the first centuries after Jesus' disciples. The Lord showed me sixteen years ago that one day, a young man with a bleeding heart would find my dwelling, and he would be the Chosen Steward of the mystery I've begun passing on to you."

Leo chuckled. "Believe me, I'm not a Chosen Steward, and I can't be the only guy with a wounded soul. How many came before me?"

Johnny shook his head. "Leo, nobody finds my dwelling. God hides it—unless He really wants someone to find me."

"Yeah, yeah. How many?"

"You don't get this. In sixteen years, many have passed by my crevice without seeing it, but you're the first to ever set foot inside here. Bikki has faithfully brought me a cookie each day, but never has he brought me a young man."

Leo's heart throbbed. Did God really see him? He wasn't someone special.

"The Lord made me wait sixteen years for you. Can't tell you how many times I've asked how much longer, if I heard Him correctly, or if He simply wanted to teach me something. But I know now He wanted to imprint on me a message about you, little prophet. The Lord told me to hand down to you the mystery of the Divine Calendar."

Leo looked up from his journal. "Divine Calendar?"

"For centuries, mankind has only known fractions. But the Lord taught me, His most unworthy servant, this mystery long ago. God wants you to experience its power and help other souls. This will, in the Lord's perfect timing, assist the fulfillment of the current phase of history, bringing the world to the next station. I'm here to teach you, son—I know you can't comprehend this, but the Lord has ordained me as your spiritual father." Johnny beamed again. "Like it or not, you're stuck with me for a while."

The radiating joy from across the table was impossible to resist. "You're my spiritual father? Didn't even know I needed one."

"Does it make you happy?"

Leo chortled. "Well, I . . . I mean, you're a nice man, but . . . I've just been out climbing all weekend and was on my way home, when . . . you know. And I have work tomorrow."

"Don't fear, Leo. Your life will continue, just down a prepared path. No more trailblazing."

Leo didn't know if he felt flattered or nervous, but Johnny did promise he would help him get home—and he seemed to be a man of his word. He shook his hand loose and grabbed the pen. "So . . . what's this calendar about?"

"God has sovereign control over the world without compromising our free will."

"How does that work?"

"Let's just say God is a master conductor of everything that happens. Time lies visibly before Him, from beginning to end. Every good choice according to His will and every evil choice against His will—nothing passes without His knowledge, and yet He never violates our freedom. There's a master plan behind *everything* that happens—whether good or evil—and that includes everything that has happened in your life as well."

Except for Johnny, the rustic room seemed to fade. "God entered our world two thousand years ago as the Proto-Man." Leo glanced at the icon on the wall and his spiritual father nodded. "Jesus lived exactly according to God's master plan for humanity, and after He returned to Heaven, He gave us the ability to enter His life—the Proto-Life."

"You mean by faith, right? Following in Jesus's footsteps? I've learned that."

"Little prophet, here lies the hidden mystery of the Divine Calendar. Jesus lived the fullness of human life, so we can enter His life experience—literally. Jesus' life was so rich, it included all our life's experiences. We can unite every day of our life with a day in Jesus' life and receive divine energy—the Proto-Life—to master our own experiences as if Jesus filled our shoes. What happens when we connect a personal incident with a matching event in Jesus' life?"

Leo shrugged, writing ferociously. "We live super righteous?"

"Oh, more than behavior. It's a transformation from the inside. You *become* heavenly. Life and light fill you and you become what Adam lost at the beginning of our history. You become whole, like the Prototype for humanity, Jesus Christ. The Proto-Life heals even the most traumatic wounds—forever gone. Every single day Jesus lived, every conversation, situation, and act summarizes the circumstances of humanity. Jesus lived our lives on our behalf."

The sealed scroll before him attracted Leo's attention, but he continued writing.

"During the first centuries after Jesus, the Holy Spirit gave the spiritual leaders a divine pattern to map out the events in Jesus' life. Instead of seasons defined by the weather, the happenings in Jesus' life formed eight spiritual seasons of salvation in this Divine Calendar.

"That means, Leo, you can unite this day to an event that happened to Jesus, and release His divine power, the Proto-Life, and transform this day into the fullness of God's purpose for you. Access the Proto-Life, and you'll understand God's mind for this distance of your life's train journey."

Leo's hand hurt, but he ignored it. "Sounds complicated. So what about my day today?"

Johnny seemed to study him and waved a finger. "Your cunningness, Leo . . . At twelve, Jesus and His family visited the temple in Jerusalem. After the feast, His parents departed to go home, convinced their Boy was among their relatives. But Jesus lingered in the temple. When His anxious parents found Him, though being on His own mission, He didn't resist and returned home with them. However, Jesus' submission to His mother later birthed understanding in her heart about His mission in Jerusalem. Now, open your hands, little prophet."

He obeyed immediately, and Johnny closed his eyes. "We're currently in the spiritual season when Jesus sends his Holy Spirit to equip His children with gifts for their mission. Let's pray.

"Our Lord Jesus, look with mercy upon Your servant, Leo. I pray he may increase in wisdom and stature, and in favor with Your Father, his mother, and all people."

Leo's angst over not getting home in time dissolved, and the lofty words Johnny taught about this mysterious calendar somehow cleared his mind.

"Give Leo the light from Your blessed youth, Jesus. Guide him for the rest of this day. Open his eyes to see the Map. Amen."

Leo lit up, flipping through the handwritten pages. "So . . . the Divine Calendar helps me unite this day with one of Jesus's days, so I can receive the Proto-Life? And this Life, which is the life Jesus lived, makes me understand God's purpose for this day on the train of time?"

Johnny grinned. "Our Heavenly Father was right about you. Imagine you've only lived your life in black and white. God wants to paint your days with heavenly colors so you would understand why things are happening."

Leo skimmed over a page. "And when the Proto-Life has restored enough people, God will forward history toward a new station?"

"Exactly. But that would make *you* a Chosen Steward of the mystery of the Divine Calendar." Johnny lifted the papyrus scroll. "Pull the string."

The red thread loosened and the seal dropped.

"Even though the eight spiritual seasons are universal patterns to understand our life through Jesus' days, there's a unique spiritual journey for everyone through the same seasons."

"Do you know your own journey, Johnny?"

"Oh, Leo. Jesus' life has become my own. It is no longer I who live, but Jesus lives through me. I think you've already felt that, am I right? I know only a little about what your future holds, but I know I have much to show you." He opened the scroll. "Can we start here?"

"What's this?!"

"It's the Legend of your Divine Calendar."

Chapter 4

THE MAP OF THE KINGDOM

"Can you see anything, Leo?" Johnny held the papyrus unrolled on the table.

Leo gaped. This surpassed any state-of-the-art 3D display. In vibrant colors, the scroll showed the universe with planet Earth revolving in the center. Everything looked different. Instead of endless blackness, space sparkled in white, illumined from golden stars, and the sun and moon seemed to hide in the brightness—if there at all.

He rose to look from another angle, and other parts of the white-golden cosmos came into view. Like a window, the scenery existed in a deeper dimension on the paper. "That's the coolest thing I've ever seen." Leo reached toward the papyrus. "Can I . . . ?"

His spiritual father nodded, and Leo's hand sunk into the scroll. "No way." Warm texture rubbed his fingers as the Earth rotated in his hand. The oceans felt like silk, and the mountain ranges, plains, and deserts brushed his skin like a rotating impasto painting. Far from any hologram, this representation contained matter.

Leo withdrew his hand, and a thin net of pulsating bluish light appeared above the continents. Streams of crystal blue formed knots with other streams, and in a few places, these rivers of sapphire merged into transparent lakes. "What is this?"

Johnny folded his hands under his chin. "Glory be to our kind Lord. He opened your eyes to see more than I prayed for. I received this map from Heaven long ago."

Leo stared. "Really?! You mean, an angel came?"

Johnny chuckled. "Spot on, little prophet. Archangel Gabriel visited me."

"No way!"

"He handed me several. Since you see what's on this scroll, this is yours."

"For me?!" Leo sat. From a distance, the blue glow formed transparent oceans in the familiar shapes of China, Iran, Israel, and a few other nations. An azure blanket also covered the US, but fainter. Leo couldn't wait to show this to his brother.

Johnny tapped his shoulder. "Only you can see what's on there. You're looking at the map of the Kingdom of God as it looks today. It's not a geographical map, but a spiritual one. Time and space restrict our age but not the spiritual realm, so the map presents itself in various forms. Sometimes as a garden, a city, or a field. In the Lord's mercy, He gave you an image you easily understand."

Leo pointed. "It's zooming in." As the scroll's window moved closer to the Earth, myriads of tiny blue stars appeared on the continents.

"The bluish lights are the Spirit of God in human souls," Johnny said, "and the rivers binding the stars are the unity of love. That's why you see such diversity of stars and hubs tied with varying intensities of light."

The scroll moved in on North America, and while the landscape looked similar, the density of the Spirit-stars took the shapes of cities and roads, like a satellite image of the continent at night.

"Johnny . . ." The man of God gestured to keep watching as they moved farther toward the surface. Leo recognized Los Angeles, Phoenix, and Denver. From a few glittering clouds, something white flashed by with angelic singing voices.

"Don't be afraid, little prophet. I see the Lord allows you to see only the Kingdom of Light. You can't see the activity of Darkness. Every blue sparkle across the continent is God's dwelling in His children, like you and me."

The window of view entered a cloud. The landscape below morphed into a heavenly scene. Streets, buildings, and parks shone in gold, the blue lights flared into gemstones, and blooming autumn-colored grasslands and waterfalls draped canyons and deserts. Before Leo could process the beauty, they exited the glorious cloud and the celestial outlook, and headed toward the rocky ravines northeast of the city of Kayenta, Arizona.

Leo touched Johnny's arm. "Why are we heading toward where we—?" A golden star radiated out of a mountainside. He leaned back as rays fanned into the cabin's ceiling like northern lights. The scroll's window was heading toward a crack in the mountain, burning like the sun, and a hint of blue emerged. Leo squinted.

"I didn't expect the Lord would show you all this," Johnny said. "He's making a point." The golden radiance intensified, hiding Johnny behind wafting rays. "Remember this, little prophet, because you won't see this again for quite some time."

"What point?" The golden light immersed the scroll and filled the room with sunlight. Leo shielded his eyes.

"Nor will they say, 'See here' or 'See there,'" Johnny said.

The gentle heat vanished, and Leo lowered his arm. Only dimmed sapphire-blue glowed in the scroll.

Johnny pointed at himself and at Leo. "For indeed, the Kingdom of God is within you."

"What do you mean?"

"God vividly displayed for you how His reign looks at this point in history. Take another glimpse in the scroll."

The papyrus showed a silver outline of a man with shoulder-length hair, and on its head and in the lower chest glowed the gentle blue light, like those all over the Kingdom Map. A golden ring encircled the figure, passing through eight symbols evenly spaced around the profile but too hazy to interpret. On the bottom left appeared a foggy table of nine symbols with "Legend" written above in gold.

Leo glanced down at his chest. No glow. Who could blame him for checking?

Johnny grinned. "You're right. That illustration is of you. Another image of God's Kingdom, but of your soul and inner man."

Leo concealed it with his hands. "Is that how you've been reading my thoughts?"

His spiritual father shook his head. "You can remove your hands. Only you can see what's there. The Lord graciously allowed me to see what you saw of the Universal Kingdom Map, but I can't see what you see now."

Blue radiance highlighted Leo's hands. "Do you see this light?"

"Only by reading your face. However, I know the design of such maps. As I said, in our age, the Kingdom of God manifests in our soul. But this scroll is more than a map of your inner self. The Legend shows the progress of your personal journey through the Divine Calendar. You see eight symbols around the temple, right?"

"Temple?"

"Oh, you have a silhouette, don't you? Do you have eight blurred symbols around the outline of your soul?"

Leo put the scroll in his lap and tried to interpret the symbols.

"Believe me, little prophet. The Holy Spirit will unveil them when you pass through the seasons in the Divine Calendar. Your Kingdom Map illustrates what happens in your soul, and the Legend will clear up, explaining those symbols. Protect it as the treasure map over your life."

"Will it show if I encounter the Proto-Life?"

"Oh, with great detail. You won't miss it."

"Does every Christian have one? The few I know in my Bible group never showed me theirs."

Johnny stretched out his arms, beaming. "Every human being experiences what's on this map. But a Chosen Steward, like you, gets a Kingdom Map. You need to know this mystery inside out so you can pass it on to others." The long-haired man leaned over the table, tapping on the scroll. "Don't tell anyone about your personal Legend, even if an angel should appear to you. God called you to teach the principles, but this scroll doesn't belong to this age. Understand?"

Leo nodded fervently.

"If you reveal what others can't see on this scroll, you'll see an empty Egyptian paper reed from that day on."

Leo swallowed, zipped his mouth with his finger, and wrote with big letters in his journal.

"Exactly. This is between you and the One who so tenderly fashioned you. When your training is over, and God sends people your way ready to receive the mysteries of the Divine Calendar, you'll know how to hand it down without compromising your personal Legend. What did the blue light in your core look like—any shape?"

Leo bent over the scroll. A dull gray filled the inside of his silver figure except for the little pulsating flame on his head and below the chest—a tiny glow with no particular shape. "It looks like—"

"Don't." Johnny placed a finger over his mouth. "Not even if an angel . . ."

"Are you testing me?"

"Little prophet, God sent me to train you."

Leo placed the scroll carefully back on the table. This certainly wasn't the plan for his weekend. He was supposed to attend his Bible-study group this evening, and work for another week to tear off a piece of his probation-countdown picture.

This afternoon was unquestionably on his top-three list of the craziest things to ever happen to him. But he had to admit Johnny was the real deal, and God was terrifyingly tangible and active. And what could he say about that supernatural image of his soul glowing on the table?

Even though this was all far above his head, he would be stupid not to believe Johnny—the man's prayer healed his ribs . . . And not only had he been surprised when Johnny declared himself as his spiritual father, but Leo had an unfamiliar feeling—security.

But a loud voice inside told him not to sell his soul to something he couldn't walk back from. Was it common sense or fear? Leo didn't know. He was still young. If he said yes to this training, what about his own dreams for the future? Would Johnny allow him to chicken out now?

But again, if the Legend could show how to heal his deeply wounded soul, and he said no to Johnny, he knew only a day or two would pass before he climbed down into the crevice to tell Johnny he'd changed his mind. However, the most glaring problem was how could he—a poorly educated summit seeker from Arizona's Up North, a baby Christian and recent criminal—be a Steward? Let alone a Chosen one?

Leo closed his eyes, shaking his head. He had to face it. There was no way back. He couldn't leave now. "If I believe I'm your Chosen Steward, what do you expect me to do?"

The hairy man leaned forward and touched his shoulder, clearly to get eye contact and search his soul again. But this time, he invited Johnny's gaze—as long as he stayed away from that sore spot.

"Ready to be equipped for your call, Leo?"

"Equipped with what?"

"You didn't expect I would let you out that door with only a scroll and a prayer of blessing, did you?"

"I kinda hoped not."

Johnny closed his eyes and Leo felt warmth in his heart. In his Legend, the blue light in his soul's core blazed, and the light on the head intensified. A thin blue line emerged around his figure, the outline of a faint sphere. He felt strangely at home, and his confidence in Johnny gave him courage.

"Ready?" Johnny said, his eyes wet.

Leo touched his heart. "I think I am."

From a drawer, Johnny grabbed a wooden canister with a leather strap attached. He popped it open. "Smell this."

He inhaled a fresh sweet-spicy aroma he almost could taste.

"Made it from the top of the juniper's stem that a storm snapped long ago. It's a gift for your Legend."

"Really?! I love it." Carefully, Leo rolled his scroll, slid it into the cylinder, and strapped it onto his back.

"That's the biggest grin I've seen on your face, Leo. Tells me you're ready to be trained in receiving God's mysteries—and to *see*."

"See what?"

Johnny tapped on Leo's journal. "Write what you have learned. When you're done, I'll show you."

Outside the window, the horizon was absorbing the orange fireball, setting the mountainous desert aflame. Kneeling beside each other on Johnny's prayer bench, Leo helped him remove the burned-out wax candles.

"What's up with all these vials?"

"That's holy water."

"Oh. And who's on all these icons?"

"My heavenly family and friends. This is my photo album." Johnny put new incense on the white charcoal. "And yours as well."

Leo plucked wax from his fingers. "So . . . you pray to them?"

The man of God placed two Bibles on the handrest in front of them. "Pray to them? Why would I do that? I talk to them, like you talk with your family."

"Oh . . . yeah. 'Course you do."

"So, there's a slight challenge to what we're about to do, and I don't know how to fix it. And that's your clothes."

Leo looked down at his fire-resistant outfit with silver and blue racing lines. "My boss gave it to me when they offered me a special deal to buy my precious Polaris. I think he must compete with my brother about who loves me the most—after Mom, of course."

"Must be a good man."

"Yeah. I don't deserve it, but he's always been so caring of me and trained me well. The mechanics come to the reception desk almost every day to ask me for advice. Started in the service hall when I was only fourteen, you know. Used to fix cars in my dreams. Love anything on wheels that goes faster than I run."

"Your boss helped you buy your car?"

"Car? Johnny, you've been great, but it's not a car. It's the most ruthless side-by-side on the market with a touch of madness, some artistry, and loads of shameless obsession with perfection. How could I afford the thirty-three grand unless Volkswagen helped me? Come to think of it, it's strange this hasn't stressed me out, but it's leaking oil up there."

Johnny tapped his back. "Don't worry. Bikki is watching over it."

Leo snorted. "What a relief."

"We have to do something about your appearance. I'll blend in, but you . . . we'll figure it out."

"So, what are we doing?"

His spiritual father opened the two Bibles. "Where do you think we'll find the Proto-Life?"

"In the Bible?"

"In the story about the Proto-Man, Jesus Christ. You saw the Spirit of God as blue lights on the Universal Kingdom Map and in your soul. This Holy Book isn't just ink on paper, but words of spirit and life. Men and women of past generations recorded the most important events for all of humanity. That's what we call the Bible. So, the Scriptures are now your second treasure map."

"To find what?"

"To encounter the Proto-Life, of course. From this day on, view the Bible as the access point to the most important events in human history. But more than that. If you immerse yourself in these texts, the Spirit within these words nurtures your soul, and the Legend displays your growth. And once your Legend is fully revealed . . ." Johnny closed his eyes. "The Legend reveals the purpose of your life and how God used your past to prepare you."

The hermit seemed to pray. Smoke from the incense holder curled and the candles danced. Leo tightened the canister belt across his chest. He enjoyed the feeling it gave him—like a samurai sword or quiver of arrows.

"I need to take you under my Spirit wings," the hermit said. "Jesus wants to show you something and needs you to come with me. He has a task for you already."

"I'm not following—take us where?"

Johnny's eyes beamed. "Before the Spirit gifts you to enter His eyewitness, you must come with me. But I have to warn you."

"About what?"

"The gifts for my call are much higher than yours, so don't panic."

Leo made sure he had zipped his suit all the way up. "I will, if you don't say what's going to happen soon."

"Ok, little prophet. Let's open First Kings one, verse ten."

After fumbling, Leo found the verse: "But he did not invite Nathan the prophet, Benaiah, the mighty men, or Solomon his brother." He looked at Johnny. "Kind of cryptic."

THE MAP OF THE KINGDOM

Johnny touched Leo's Bible. "I'll pray to make this as easy as possible, but I can't promise a safe landing. Read this verse slowly again and again. Try to absorb the verse, comprehend the words, and receive the impressions of the Spirit. If a phrase or word stands out, like a little light in your mind, zoom in and focus only on that part. Continue until you're left with one truth. Then ask Jesus to reveal Himself to you."

Leo nodded. Strangely enough, he felt the phrase "did not" leaped at him each time he read. But nothing else came to him. *Ah, I've got to ask.* "Jesus, can You please—"

The cabin quaked. He grabbed Johnny, but his spiritual father still knelt, eyes closed. "Johnny!" He shook his side. "Did you feel that!?" The man continued to pray as if nothing was happening.

In the window, a white light appeared on the horizon, absorbing the sun and moving toward them. "Johnny!" The sky and clouds disappeared into the brightness as it swept over the mesas and buttes. The walls blew out, the roof lifted, and a golden-fiery ring descended toward him, dissolving the sandstone crevice, the hovering cabin pieces, and the juniper tree in a whirling motion.

Leo felt hyperalert. Strangely enough, Johnny—still kneeling next to him with eyes closed—filled him with peace while the dazzling inferno sucked the shredded world into its center.

A mighty gust—a breath from above—sent every grain of sand exploding in all directions as the ring blazed on all sides. Paralyzed in wonder, a word seemed to be placed on his lips. "Holy," he whispered. The brilliant circle lifted and left nothing but the purest whiteness.

Hay appeared between his knees. Leo reached for Johnny but grasped a wooden pole. He sat in a pile of straw, apparently in a wooden cage of sorts. "Johnny?!" Gone.

Chapter 5

ANYWHERE BUT UTAH

A canopy of animal skin shielded Leo from the sun in the earthy-smelling wagon. Straw poked his palms as he sat in damp hay and absorbed the rocking from the road.

The rattling from horsemen and chariots mixed with conversations in a foreign language flowed between the side boards. Leo's eyes adapted to the sunlight beaming through an opening above the tailgate, revealing a parade of riders, villagers dressed in cloaks, and farmers leading oxen and donkeys. Shepherds with their sheep traveled in the fields below. Shrubs and olive trees passed by on one side of the timeworn country road, a low stone wall on the other, and an ancient fortified city faded into the distance. Leo was anywhere but in Utah.

He squeezed hay in his hand. Where or *when* was he? Leo pinched himself. "Ouch." Was this real?! He knew he ought to be losing his mind, but some miracle kept him composed. He closed his eyes. *God is in control. God has full control. God won't—*

The cart bumped, oxen bellowed, and he tipped over, hitting his Legend canister against the sideboards. Quickly, he slid the cylinder over his shoulder and searched for damage, but Johnny's handicraft proved solid.

"Where are you, Johnny?" Leo whispered, spitting out a strand of straw. He crawled up front. Two yoked bulls pulled his cart, led by two men—neither resembled his mentor.

"Boh!" a gruff voice said, and donkeys brayed as another wagon squeezed past carrying bowls, enormous knives, and meat forks. The cortege approached a hillside housing mud brick homes with walled courtyards, flat roofs, and laundry flapping in the burning wind.

Johnny would easily blend in, but Leo couldn't spot his fiery golden eyes anywhere.

He rolled onto his back. *Okay. Stay cool . . . Chosen Steward training . . . it's training, nothing dangerous.* He dried his forehead.

"Eifo haMelech Shlomo?" a man shouted repeatedly, and Leo sat up. Was that Hebrew? A wanderer with an unshaved face and filthy clothes, heading in the opposite direction, grabbed at the passing travelers, but they pushed him away.

Hoofs trotted and a rider snatched a spear from a chariot. Before Leo could process the scene, an efficient bone-snapping thrust pierced the man. The wanderer dropped to his knees, and Leo hid his face, hands shaking. Shouting and screaming drowned the man's gurgling. Metal sang, followed by a wet sound, and something dropped to the ground. Leo spread his fingers. The soldier kicked the body off the road, sending it rolling into dry bushes. The spear's scarlet tip glinted in his hand.

"Help me, God," Leo whispered, pulling up his knees. "Get me out of here."

"*Does King David know Adonijah will be anointed?*" said a traveler to another close to his wagon.

Leo cocked his head. But that was English . . . or did his ears just interpret their Hebrew?

"*Guess so,*" another man answered. "*I tagged along 'cause I heard he rewards those gathering outside En Rogel. Adonijah should have access to silver, you know.*"

Carefully, Leo peeked between the boards.

"*You're in it for the money?! That's what I feared . . . I feel bad about the whole thing. The king is old all right, but he hasn't rested with his fathers yet.*"

"*Guess the young man's eager to sit on his father's throne.*"

"*But didn't the king say Solomon would sit on his throne?*"

What a miracle. Somehow, he understood Hebrew. "But I need moral support, God," Leo said silently. "Please, take me to Johnny."

"*Thought so too,*" the other man said. "*But did you notice that mighty one with the bloody spear?*"

"*That's Commander Joab, isn't he?*"

The local nodded and pointed up ahead. "*And that priest up there, that's Abiathar. So King David must know. Guess he changed his mind. You know, he's got a few to pick from. And frankly, Adonijah's got the looks. Even Solomon can't compete with that black mane.*"

"*Yeah, but . . . what about the promises?*"

"*What promises?*"

"*The king said Solomon should build the House of the Lord, not Adonijah.*"

"*Well . . . guess God changed His mind as well.*"

The man jabbed the other's shoulder. *"You Philistine. That's blasphemy."*

"You know what?" the local said, rubbing his shoulder. *"See this?"*

The other bent toward him, and a blow to his face sent him reeling into the wagon. Leo rolled into the middle of the hay as horsemen arrived. Through the opening above the tailgate, Leo watched the soldiers separate the brawling men. A charioteer forced them to walk on opposite sides, apparently mediating.

Leo closed his eyes. "What am I doing here?" Johnny told him God had a task for him, but he heard Fred's voice echoing: *Only men with confidence grow a goatee.* Leo fiddled with his beard. Oh, he was confident. Perhaps it wasn't the morally right thing to do, but it required guts to put his Polaris in reverse and fill Fred's mouth with gravel, trusting he could beat the Jeep on public roads. He sat up, clenching his fists. "I have confidence—just need the right type."

"Shalom. Ma shemcha?" a girl said from a man's shoulders to a traveler with a donkey carrying firewood. A lady quieted the girl and Leo could only hear the foreign language as the conversation continued.

Leo shifted in the hay to hear better. He couldn't make out a word. "Why can't I understand them anymore, God? What am I supposed to do?"

"Ha'im Adoniyahu yida'eg livnot the Lord's temple?" one man leading his cart said.

Leo raised his head. "Are you kidding me?" He crawled up front.

"Perhaps—after he's built his own palace," the other answered.

"Should we tell King David?"

The other put his finger to his lips, shaking his head. *"Not if you want to lie down tonight with your head attached."* The exchange continued, but incomprehensibly in the foreign tongue.

He covered his ears to block out the buzzing. What would be the right thing to do? A thought hit him and goosebumps crawled up his back. "No, God. Don't make me do this." The wagon's cover waved in the breeze. "I'm not *that* confident . . ." But the thought persisted, and Leo threw herbage over his racing boots—he'd be easier to spot than a blind man behind a steering wheel.

Leo grabbed his cylinder and opened the scroll. A faint sphere enclosed the silver figure of his soul, and watching it filled him with the same peace as being close to Johnny.

Gently, he touched the projection of his soul. Warm and soft—how surreal, an illustration of his invisible self. How could it not fascinate him?

Shimmers appeared above his soul's head, and Leo carefully withdrew his fingertip. Glimmer rained over the figure's head and shoulders. He glanced left and right, but no sparkles.

Leo exhaled—instead of wrestling with the thought God must have sent, he embraced it. In the silhouette's head, a white star emerged. *No way. This is for real.* The light glowed so distinctly that shadows flickered on the wagon walls. What if he could actually do what this thought suggested? In the scroll, the brilliant light descended halfway toward his heart. He touched his chest, feeling an intangible warmth.

The more he believed in his abilities—with God's help—the more the bright star approached the silhouette's heart, and sparkles poured over his soul. He ran a hand through his dark locks, disappointed not to see drizzling glitter. But he knew exactly what to do—and he believed he could pull it off.

Leo closed his eyes and sighed.

From a distance, shouting arose, and Leo slid the Legend into the canister and tightened it to his back. He peeked up ahead. The procession congregated on open land outside the Middle Eastern village. A rounded stone, waist-high, stood in the center, and horsemen chased away local youth who seemed set on moving the landmark.

Leo rose and wrestled with the first knot that tied the wagon's cover to the slats. Ahead, soldiers directed wagons carrying wood, slaughtering tools, and animals in sections across the field. Carpenters brought premade pieces of a platform and nailed them together.

Finally, the first side of the beige cover hung into the wagon, scorching hot on the top. By the time Leo untied the third row of knots, the wagon was circling the stone. With sore fingers, he tackled the remaining knots. Conversations hummed in the local tongue, but the bleating and mooing told Leo what he needed to know. Even though he'd never felt deeply bonded to animals, he didn't want to witness the slaughtering.

As his wagon halted, the cover released and dropped onto his head. He stepped on the skin and pulled, tearing a seam, and folded the blistering sides against each other. The sun had softened the pelt, and Leo tied it around his neck, concealing his racing suit and Legend tube. He rubbed hay in his hair and soil in his face, hoping to look like a weathered beggar.

The owners of the wagon chatted while heading around the cart. As the tailgate fell open, Leo threw hay into their faces and jumped outside. Bright daylight flashed, blinding him. Leo tripped into what felt like tools and dove headlong. The men yelled and wooden handles rattled. Hebrew words—foul ones, he figured—showered him.

Hands of iron grabbed his shoulders, lifted him to his feet, and bound him. But Leo snapped through the rope around his neck and ran, leaving them with their property—and his disguise. Great, he'd sanded his fingertips for nothing. People probably thought he'd fallen from the moon.

He fled between rows of wagons. At the far end, riders leaned against their chariots and drank. Leo rolled under a cart. Adrenaline rushed while he scanned the area for any sort of fabric. Close to some carpenters lay a brown outer garment over a pile of crates.

On all fours, Leo spun forward beneath the loads. Someone shouted. A dozen carts behind knelt the two men, shaking their fists. Leo rolled out on the opposite side. He felt the stares, but walked toward the garment as if it belonged to him and snatched it. Hurrying between piles of firewood, he slid behind a curtain shading jars of water and wrapped himself in the garment as best as he knew how. Leo exhaled, emerged calmly, and headed for the road.

The owners of his wagon yelled—or perhaps someone else—hardly distinguishable amidst the noise of woodworkers, animal slaughter, and competing conversations. He maneuvered past piles of timber and hay, excused himself through a circle of talkative jar-carrying women, and paced beside a long row of parked chariots.

Leo peeked over his shoulder. Workers carried a table and an ornamented chair onto the platform amidst the sea of inhabitants, animals, and equipment.

The people he passed stared at him, some with disgust, moving children out of his way as he stepped onto the road. The procession poured onto the field while armored horsemen advanced down the road. Leo swallowed, knowing he was the only one heading in the opposite direction. Fixing his gaze on the dusty road, he walked as far to the side as he could.

Horseshoes clapped and intimidating shadows passed by. The soldiers' glares pierced him. A rider said something, but Leo shook his head, keeping his eyes to the ground. The metal rattling never ended as the armed mountains blocked the sun. Another rider spoke, and Leo discreetly shook his head. The rider hollered, clearly angry, and Leo stopped. The soldier spat and dust swirled before Leo's feet.

Apparently, Leo caught the interest of two mounted warriors pulling a larger carriage. Two dozen riders halted and formed a line behind them. The soldiers wore ornamented tunics, bronze breastplates, greaves, and helmets. They carried a shield and quiver on their backs, a bow around their shoulders, and a sword sheathed at their sides. Two enormous stallions trotted close to the carriage, all bearing royal lion insignias. A broad-shouldered horseman with a scar across his face signaled Leo to approach.

The man spoke Hebrew and Leo shrugged, pointing at his lip. "D-don't understand what you say, sir." The warrior continued speaking, and Leo shook his head. "I'm s-sorry, sir. American." The soldier shouted something at the carriage.

The vehicle opened and a hand beckoned Leo to come. His heart throbbed as he walked past the sturdy horse legs. Thoughts of arrows planted deeply in his back kept him from leaping over the draft pole and fleeing into the field.

Leo stopped before the open carriage. A handsome man sat wearing an embroidered robe and jewelry, holding a crown on his lap. His pitch-black locks covered his shoulders, and the cleft in his chin highlighted his well-trimmed beard. This had to be the supplanter, Adonijah. Why would such a royal entertain a destitute young man? Perhaps the hint of his Southern slang sounded exotic? Or maybe impressing a traveler from a faraway country excited this man's ego?

The kingly man stretched out his gemstone-adorned hand. What was more sickening? Kissing Adonijah's hand or arrows sinking into his back?

Leo pointed at his workman's robe and dirty hair. "Oh, I'm not worthy." Shaking his head, Leo took a step back. "I'm just a poor kid. Don't want to s-smudge your diamonds, sir."

Adonijah lowered his hand, narrowing his eyebrows. *"Speak Hebrew. Where are you from?"*

Leo stuttered—suddenly understanding Hebrew again—but regained his composure and shrugged. "Arizona. Don't speak your language, sir. I'm just a tourist, trying to find my relative out here somewhere." Leo hoped his incomprehensible English would prove he wasn't from a nation they viewed as a threat.

"Are you a spy? Where are you going?"

Leo peeked at the horsemen. Not a chance to escape these guys—diplomacy was his safe way out. He searched his pockets, feeling his New Testament. What about his Polaris keys, insurance slip, or wallet? If only he hadn't launched his phone at Bikki. How about his cheap analogue watch?

Leo loosened his forty-dollar online purchase and offered it, staring at the ground. "Please accept this as a gift instead."

Adonijah snatched the watch, examined it, and held it to his ear. *"Egyptian? No . . . What does it do?"*

Leo pointed to his wrist and the usurper struggled with the tiny pin. Stepping backwards, Leo bowed repeatedly.

The royal leaned back, waving him off. *"The peasant doesn't speak our language!"* Adonijah called out. *"Let him go!"* The king's son kept Leo's watch, and the escort continued toward the noisy crowd.

Leo exhaled as the riders left. The lines of soldiers, wagons, and inhabitants that had piled up moved along. It seemed like his encounter with Adonijah had gained everyone's approval.

Chapter 6

HEAVENLY BLUEPRINTS

The wind carried the sound of harps and blaring shofars from Adonijah's assembly, and in the opposite direction, the ancient fortified city crowned a hill. Miraculously, God had enabled Leo to eavesdrop on conversations about the usurper's plot to steal the throne from Solomon—both sons of King David. Leo didn't grasp all the implications, but God wanted him to tell the king about the rebellion, and he had no plans of failing his first Chosen Steward training.

Sweat ran down his back and thirst scorched his throat. Between some rustling olive trees bubbled a spring. Leo wiped his forehead, lifted his face, and closed his eyes. Maybe this was all a hallucination? When he woke up this morning in his camping tent by the Bears Ears, he had mumbled a few psalms from the Bible while rubbing his eyes. Now, just some hours later, he was looking for the Psalmist himself. He would be committed to a hospital if he ever told anyone.

Hooves galloped from behind, and Leo turned, backing into a ditch. A mounted warrior pulled the reins, and the armored white stallion skidded to a dusty halt. Sunshine reflected in the polished bronze. "Ir David?"

Leo stuttered, shielding his eyes before the regal figure.

The horseman pointed up the road. "Tzarich hasa'ah?" He offered his hand.

Leo gaped. "Are you giving me a ride?!"

The rider chuckled and answered in Hebrew.

"Man, I don't know how to. I mean, I've tried it back home, but . . ." Hoping it wasn't a trap, Leo grabbed his hand and the warrior lifted him up front.

The stallion reared onto its hind legs, and Leo clasped the robust forearms holding the reins. Blue sky and horse legs replaced the view of the road, and when the horse landed, it felt like driving his Polaris. The warrior's breastplate pressed into his back on cue, and the horse shot toward the walled city.

Firmly secured between the warrior's arms, Leo rode the stallion's gallop, moving his hips and feeling the rhythm through his body. The chuckling soldier obviously mastered this race and Leo's competitive instincts kicked in.

People cleared the road as they swooshed past gardens leading up to the first city gate. If only his off-roader had one hundred forty-four horsepower of this kind! The warrior clearly enjoyed making sure Leo wouldn't easily forget this ride. Hopefully, the soldier would never find out Leo was about to alert the king about Adonijah. The sovereignty of God pulled him out of the thrill, quieting him—this had to be His working.

The wind nudged his outer garment until a sudden gust ripped it away. Behind him, the warrior turned silent. *Great. Now what?* They slowed to a trot and turned left toward the southern gate. People stared at Leo's suit, shining like silver in the sunlight.

The hooves clattered against the cobblestone, and the rider brought the horse to a standstill. Thankfully, he let him down. Leo bowed, feeling beaten, and tapped on his heart. The soldier watched him steadily as Leo backed and waved. Catching the eyes of everyone, he paced through the gateway.

Beige stone buildings and terraced gardens cascaded down the hillside—talk about time travel. As Leo entered a busy marketplace, a worrying silence followed his wake. Quickly, he headed toward a shaded alley. Where could he get a cloak? They probably didn't accept dollar bills, but what about coins?

He slid behind stacks of empty boxes and leaned against the wall. Fabric flapped between the roofs twenty feet above. Leo emptied his wallet, sifting through the cents to separate the shiny ones.

"I brought you these, little prophet," a voice said, as fingers lifted a crate away. A long-haired, bearded man smiled at him, eyes flaring. His dark-green outer garment, wrapped around a hairy tunic, clothed his lean figure. A brownish robe and a sash lay folded in his arms.

"Johnny! I never thought I'd find you."

"Been scouting the square since I arrived. Knew you would come." His mentor wrapped him in the new robe and tied the decorated ribbon around his waist. The silent care emanating from Johnny's presence absorbed Leo's anger at being left alone. The hermit pulled hay from Leo's hair. "Love to hear your story, but we'll do that later. Clean up your face and come."

Johnny led the way through the market. "I know who you should share your testimony with. Saw him up there moments ago. Hope he hasn't reached the palace, because I'd rather keep you anonymous."

Leo jogged up a hill after Johnny's rapid sandals and rushed past a fountain, through winding streets, up a tight stairway, and finally entered what appeared to be the main street.

"There he is," Johnny said.

Bent over with hands resting on his knees, Leo lifted his head. Under an olive tree, next to a steep stair structure, leaned a gray-haired man on his walking stick. He wore a simple turban and a deep-red outer garment, apparently lost in contemplation. "Who's that?"

"Nathan the Prophet."

"Never heard of him."

"Soon you will. Confessed your sins lately?"

Leo stood straight. "What?!"

Johnny grabbed his elbow. Before entering the shadow of the tree, his mentor bowed to the ground, startling the old man. The prophet, apparently embarrassed, tapped him with his stick, and Johnny grabbed Nathan's hands and kissed them. They spoke Hebrew until Johnny seemed to introduce Leo. "Tell the prophet what you saw, Leo. I'll translate."

Leo stammered, and Nathan's wrinkled face broke into a smile. The old man spoke and Johnny said, "He's saying, 'Peace, my son. Tell me what you saw.'"

After Leo delivered a rapid-fire narrative about the conversations he overheard in the wagon and his escape, Nathan interrupted Leo and asked about Adonijah. "The prophet says, 'Can you describe him one more time, please?'"

"Black and weighty locks, defined jaw and chin, dark eyes, lots of jewelry, and a golden crown on his lap—he wanted me to kiss his ring."

His mentor translated, and the old man sighed, looking up at the olives. "'But he did not invite me, Benaiah, the mighty men, or his brother Solomon,'" Johnny translated back.

Leo stared at the prophet and his mentor. *"Did not . . . ?"* His spiritual father winked.

"'I know this,'" Prophet Nathan continued through Johnny, "'because I just spoke with Benaiah, and Solomon is in his house. Can't believe Joab and Abiathar have gone this far—and King David is still alive.'" The prophet struck the tree with his stick. "'This is a revolt! I need to talk to Bathsheba.'"

Nathan put his hand on Leo's head. "'The God of Abraham, Isaac, and Jacob bless you, lad. No matter what nation you're from, the God of Israel loves those who fear Him—'" Suddenly, Nathan withdrew his hand as if he had burned himself. His eyes below his bushy eyebrows seemed to examine Leo until the prophet finally spoke: "'And you're a servant of our coming Messiah. You're an Israelite indeed, and—you're a chosen steward of the treasures of the Kingdom of Heaven.'"

Prophet Nathan kissed Leo's head, embraced Johnny, kissing his cheeks, and left them.

Leo stared after him. The prophet's last words went deep, real deep. He felt utterly unworthy—and appreciated, no . . . loved. Leo pulled out the Legend from the canister. A white light danced in the blue flame in the silhouette's core, bursting rays into his mind. Slowly, he rolled up the scroll. "Think Jesus just gave me some of His Proto-Life."

Johnny grinned. "The shimmer in your eyes confirms it, little prophet."

"Really?! Can you see it?"

"Come now. Let's get a spot with a direct view before everybody comes."

His mentor took him along the city wall, through an arch, and down a slope where women carried water jars.

Leo nudged Johnny's weathered cloak. "It feels like you know what's going to happen."

"That's why you want to read your Bible. Wait and see."

They turned by a tower, descended a stair to a pool, and sat by the water with a view toward the city.

"Why did God do this to me, Johnny?"

"Called you as a Chosen Steward?"

"Well, that too. But I've never seen a man murdered before. I was terrified, you know. Why did God drop me into the wagon? Had to figure out everything without you."

"He prompted you just enough to make you feel the need to act."

"Yeah. But why?"

Johnny looked him in the eyes. "To show you that you *can* do the right thing. God wants you to see in yourself what He sees."

In the clear water, Leo's reflection stared back at him. He sighed. The good or the bad? Was there any good in him at all? He kicked a pebble into the pool and Johnny shook his finger.

"And King David said," Johnny uttered, apparently reciting Scripture. "'Call to me Zadok the priest, Nathan the prophet, and Benaiah the son of Jehoiada.' So they came before the king. The king also said to them, 'Take with you the servants of your lord, and have Solomon my son ride on my own mule, and take him down to Gihon. There let Zadok the priest and Nathan the prophet anoint him king over Israel; and blow the horn, and say, 'Long live King Solomon!' Then you shall come up after him, and he shall come and sit on my throne, and he shall be king in my place. For I have appointed him to be ruler over Israel and Judah.'"

Johnny nodded toward the city wall. "Look who's coming . . ."

Leo shielded his eyes toward the sound of singing. A man in a priestly robe walked in their direction next to Prophet Nathan, who carried a horn. Behind them, a kingly figure rode a mule.

The streets thronged with rejoicing and the playing of instruments. "Long live King Solomon!" the city roared so the earth seemed to split. Leo, with ears covered, followed Johnny at the rear of the procession toward King David's palace.

Johnny grabbed Leo's arm, and they waited until the inhabitants were far ahead. "It's time to leave," Johnny whispered. "But the Lord has more to show you before we go home."

Withdrawing into an empty backstreet, Johnny took hold of Leo's hands and prayed.

A distant thunder drew nearer, and the gravel bounced until the ground rocked, knocking Leo off his feet. The sky ripped open, and a bright light rolled it up like a scroll. Like sand in the wind, stone by stone, the buildings slowly blew away from the top down. Leo screamed, but Johnny pulled him to his feet. High above, the flaring ring returned, disintegrating the landscape from the horizon, closing in on them.

As the golden circle descended, even the ground gave way, sprays of dirt flying toward it. Again, peace overcame Leo. He stood frozen in awe—or was it an inherent form of obedience that kept him gazing? "Holy, holy, holy," he whispered. In an instant, the cobblestones beneath his feet shot in every direction, the sparkling ring ascended, and brightness engulfed him.

From the indescribable whiteness emerged cedar logs, stones, and fabrics, forming a whirlwind around him. Behind Leo, two stone pillars rose. Materials clattered together into a cedar floor and wove a thick carpet beneath his feet. Plaster covered the rising walls of stone and wood, and invisible hands painted frescoes of fruitful fields. Oil lamps dropped into the hall and lit. A massive roof rumbled as it landed on columns. At last, pottery and decorative items of cedar, bronze, and ivory lined up, highlighting the way toward the massive vestibule doors that swung closed.

Leo's spiritual father, holding a wooden box, finished his request with the chamberlain. The official asked them to wait and entered the palace's main hall.

Glancing at the guards, Leo poked Johnny's side. "He sounded positive," he whispered.

"You understood us?"

"Yeah. God opened my ears."

"Good. That makes this easier."

A few minutes later, the ornamented double doors opened. "His Majesty King Solomon can receive you now. As with all unexpected guests, your audience might be brief."

They entered the throne room. The young king, wearing a red royal robe, golden crown, and a scepter across his lap, sat writing in a scroll. King Solomon looked up and called them forward, his wavy hair framing bright eyes. Leo followed Johnny's lead as they knelt, and they walked onwards. Still at a distance from the first throne step, they bowed to the ground.

The king sat clearly immersed in his writing. "Friends of my father, what can I do for you?"

They rose, and Johnny opened his wooden box with dried fruit, placing it before the throne.

"Hope you can study this one day," King Solomon said, his gaze lingering on Leo until he closed the manuscript. "Never have I felt my pen flow like this. This will become my greatest song so far—perhaps even the Song of Songs."

"Your Majesty," Johnny said. "We've traveled from afar to seek your wisdom. My disciple, Leo, and I would love to listen to your understanding about the plans of the temple your father, His Majesty King David, received from the God of Israel."

The king massaged the scepter knob. "I'm glad to hear it's known I've begun the construction. Make sure you head up to the Temple Mount before you depart. You've not seen anything like it."

"We're curious," Johnny continued, "to learn from Your Majesty's understanding of the origin of this divine revelation."

The king rested both hands on the scepter and closed his eyes. "The Spirit of the Lord is here. That assures me." He commanded the guards to leave. As the doors closed behind them, the king rose, revealing his double-edged sword in a golden scabbard. "I want to speak freely—those who love the Lord are no strangers, but some of these excellent guards are strangers to me."

"We're honored, Your Majesty," Johnny said and knelt, and Leo followed.

"Enough formalities. What do you want to know about the temple plans?"

"What is the original model?"

King Solomon nodded. "Like our great Prophet Moses, my father, King David, received earthly plans that reflect heavenly structures. These temple plans are shadows of the temple in Heaven. When I perfectly follow all these instructions and commandments, I realign my kingdom to Heaven. This agreement between Heaven and Earth allows God to dwell here, like the Garden of Eden in the beginning. No nation will conquer us if God is with us."

Johnny folded his hands, seemingly to contain himself. "So . . . these plans—or images—restore the world from the great separation at the beginning of human history?"

"Yes. God wants to live among us again."

Johnny looked at Leo, seemingly to drive a point home. "Heavenly blueprints to build God's dwelling on Earth . . ." His mentor continued. "Your Majesty, forgive me, but why do you want God to live among you?"

King Solomon laughed. "And how would your days look like if the Creator of the world was your King and Friend?"

Leo fought with himself, trying to muster enough courage. He had to tell King Solomon about his mission in Adonijah's camp.

"Your Majesty," Johnny said, "how many seasons will pass before the temple is complete?"

"Six years."

"Where do you find the manpower for such a magnificent project?"

The king pointed upward. "The Lord's mighty outstretched arm. He subdued our enemies and they serve us as a workforce and provide materials."

His spiritual father tapped on Leo's shoulder. "We're honored by Your Majesty's generous welcome. The king has put our hearts at ease. May we ask Your Majesty one last request before we leave?" Johnny glanced at Leo. "May we pray together?"

The king appeared puzzled, but agreed. Johnny and Leo knelt, and King Solomon got down in front of his seat.

"Lord God of Israel," Johnny prayed. "We thank You for sending angels onto our path, and His Majesty filled the role of one, sharing his insight. Protect the king's throne."

Leo felt King Solomon move, but he kept eyes closed.

"As you protected the king from Adonijah's takeover, protect his heart from the same."

The king had to be standing beside the throne, but a flash of white behind Leo's closed eyelids won his attention.

"And as similar angels told Prophet Nathan about the uprising, may the same angels remind His Majesty to guard the throne of his heart."

Shooting stars filled Leo's vision.

Feet stepped quickly down the throne. "Who are you?!"

"As servants of the Most High, we pray. Amen."

Whiteness enveloped Leo as a hand reached for his shoulder, but passed through him like air.

Chapter 7

THE CHOSEN STEWARD

Leo leaned against the lukewarm sandstone at the mouth of the crevice, and the first stars poked through the deep-blue above Utah's desert. His hand hurt from writing about his mission to save the throne in Israel. Surprisingly, he enjoyed journaling—it helped him think.

For the past six months, Leo had frequently plunged into a suffocating darkness that he would deny even existed within himself, but being with Johnny pierced this blackness with irresistible light. How could his soul handle such extremes? Would he implode or explode?

Home was nestled just across the border between the distant Arizonian buttes, but it felt much further away in his soul. Everything Johnny taught him lugged in the roots of his life. Leo rubbed his face, expecting at any moment to toss his duvet aside as his mom pounded on his bedroom door. If it had happened in the wagon when the horseman murdered the wanderer, he would have been relieved, but now that he had completed his first training...

The thought of this moment only being a vivid dream stirred sadness deep within. Leo admitted that this Chosen Steward role made a tiny spot in his adventure-seeking heart thrill with anticipation of the unknown. Oh, how his brother would envy his time-travel experience, but could he ever tell him? Could Leo tell anyone?

Leo rubbed his hands, breathing into them, and shuffled them deep into his pockets. In some sense, life had to go on. How would his mother and younger brother make it without him helping to pay the bills? He tried to be a role model for his brother as well. Leo liked him—he loved his mother too. But rarely did he express what their support meant to him. So often, he whispered to himself: "Be a man, show strength." What does *be a man* actually mean?

Honor and success were manly traits, weren't they? To be someone significant. Throughout his brief life, he'd learned that only hard work earned the skills needed to succeed. That's why everyone at Volkswagen Kayenta loved him now—it couldn't be any different with God. He should straighten up and be more obedient to his mother. If God was keeping track of him now as His Chosen Steward, he had to stop arguing—at least daily. Surely, God understood his frustration with his controlling mother as well.

Chilly air dropped from the edge one hundred feet above, and the moon appeared from behind a cloud. What should he do with Fred's report about him running away from the collision? The man said he would go to the police tomorrow. Would Leo lose his license—and worse, his Polaris privileges? Would his sentence be extended?

Leo sighed heavily, shaking his head. "Okay..." He glanced over his shoulder—good, Johnny was still inside the cabin. Leo knelt and folded his hands. "God, I'm serious this time. It was wrong of me to run away from Fred. Can you forgive me? Amen—in Jesus' name I pray. Amen." He rose and brushed off his knees.

Even though all this felt good and right, one massive question remained: Who was going to take him seriously? He had a criminal record—a Chosen Steward on probation. He shouldn't get too excited—what was he thinking? How could God accept him for this task?

Leo shivered. He had accepted Jesus into his heart less than three months ago, so he wasn't exactly cut out for the task, was he? Even if he wanted to be a Chosen Steward—a manly title he'd love to keep—he disqualified himself on all points. He would keep his new status for a month, and then God would fire him. Leo kicked a pebble into the canyon. *You idiot. Just because you want to be a Chosen Steward doesn't mean God will be satisfied with your performance.* He grabbed his hair. *Why am I always so naïve? I never learn—*

"Leo?" Johnny said tenderly from behind. The hermit tiptoed forward, forehead wrinkled. "You're doubting yourself. Trust me, you're doing exceptionally well. Little prophet."

"How am I supposed to do this, Johnny? I'm not a hero, and I don't have faith like you." His mentor raised his hand. "I'm a coward. Wanted to escape the wagon when I saw that bloody spear." Leo hid his face in his hands.

"Sorry you had to see that."

"You got the wrong guy."

"Little prophet, God qualified you. Remember watching the Kingdom Map? And your excitement before we traveled to Israel?"

Leo sniffed. Somehow, Johnny's words eased his frustration.

Johnny moved closer, his expression serious. "And you did well in your encounter with Adonijah—look at you."

Leo raised his eyebrows. "What's there to look at?"

"You're becoming a Chosen Steward."

"A chosen chicken."

"Chicken?" His mentor chuckled and waved him over. "It's evening and you're cold. Let's go inside." Johnny wrapped his arm around Leo's shoulder as they strolled toward the meager cottage. "You don't realize why God brought you back three thousand years, do you?"

The age-old juniper tree overhanging the cabin's rusty roof tempted Leo to ask what brought Johnny three thousand years into the future. He cleared his throat. "To warn King David about Adonijah?"

Johnny held the door. "Why then didn't God use a local?"

A lantern above the fireplace and two dozen flickering lights in the prayer corner warmly illuminated the humble abode. Across the table, behind dripping beeswax candles, sat Johnny, his face animated with dancing shadows, giving him an even wilder look.

Immersed in his own thoughts, Leo met his spiritual father's probing look. "What is it?"

His mentor rose and put a pen and paper on the table. "Can you write to your mother so she won't mobilize a search and rescue? Say it as it is. Your off-roader broke down and a friendly native welcomed you for the night. At sunrise, he can fix the oil leak so you can drive home without using your expensive insurance."

Leo's jaw dropped. He could only afford the insurance with the highest out-of-pocket fee. *How does he know all my secrets if he can't see my Legend?*

"You think that would calm her?" Johnny said.

"Yeah, but . . . do you have any tools—and oil? And how do we mail this letter?"

"Don't worry about either."

Seemingly, a tumbleweed brushed against the door and the candles wavered in the draft. Was this his chance to make it right? He grabbed the pen and wrote. A few minutes later, Leo pushed the letter across the table. "I don't trust myself. Can you read it? Does it sound like me?"

"You wouldn't know?"

"No, but apparently you would."

His mentor smiled and read. "Who's Marlo?"

"Oh, he's teaching me the piano . . ." Leo scratched his neck. "And leads the Bible study I attend around this time."

Johnny peeked over the paper. "And Angelina doesn't know?"

"Not yet . . . she isn't the religious type."

His mentor raised his eyebrows, glancing at him, and continued reading. "Sure about this, little prophet? Can't rewrite once it's mailed."

Leo sighed. "God has high hopes for me. Don't really have a choice, do I—think I'm up for it?"

Johnny waited in silence. Finally, he rolled the letter, sealing it with a drip of candle wax. "I do. And you move me." His mentor opened the door and a raven flapped inside, landing on the table.

"Bikki!" Leo said, gawking. "Forgive me!"

The black bird stepped around the candles, cocking its head. "Kiii-do thro-wing-wing. Ki-do-do wing-wing."

"It's just a bird, Leo." Bikki jumped onto Johnny's shoulder, and his mentor held the roll before the raven's feet. The glossy bird grasped the letter and flew outside.

"How will he find my house?"

Johnny closed the door and returned. "That's one clever bird. Like I said, I have no idea where he gets my cookies."

Clearly, God cared a lot for Johnny. If Leo had shown little improvement after becoming Christian, could this be hindering God from helping him like He backed Johnny? "Is there anything God can't do?"

His mentor folded his hands. "Force you to love Him."

"Oh . . . that's . . . deep."

"You still don't know why God wanted me to take you to Adonijah's rebellion."

"Johnny, I've understood ten percent of what you've told me. I'm called to help people find Proto-Life and realign the flow of history—and I have the coolest scroll displaying what happens in my soul when I do. That's about it."

"A decent start." Johnny nodded toward the journal on the table, and Leo opened a new page and clicked the pen. "Accidents, people's inner fears, spiritual confusion, and many other evils hinder men and women from impacting their community and even the world. God leads Chosen Stewards to sidetracked key souls to realign them into His purpose for them. When these souls enter their God-given role, the evil powers that derail their lives lose influence. How does the transformation of these individuals happen?"

"The Proto-Life?"

His mentor nodded. "The Life of the Proto-Man, Jesus, encompasses every event of our own lives. But more than just a good way to live, it's the specific path the Creator designed for every person. Proto-Life makes us fully human.

"Imagine God wrote a story about your life where each page is how Jesus would live your days. That's what Proto-Life looks like. This divine power restores your days to what's written in your book. History becomes the grand tale of all our lives. The more souls that abide in the stream of Proto-Life, the closer history moves toward the next station of prophetic fulfillment."

Leo looked up from the journal, feeling more upbeat. "So, God uses Chosen Stewards to release a spiritual power that helps people live out their ultimate story?"

Johnny smiled. "Here, the Divine Calendar comes into play." He placed a small icon on the table depicting twelve men sitting in a room and a dove spreading flames on their heads. "We're in the spiritual season of Pentecost when Jesus asked His Heavenly Father to send the Holy Spirit to equip His followers for their personal mission. That's how the Divine Calendar explains the Proto-Life's activity throughout the eight Seasons of Salvation. Like how our normal calendar guides us in the fieldwork needed to grow crops, so the Divine Calendar shows us what the Proto-Life does to mature our souls for the main purpose of our life."

Leo turned a page. "So the more I follow the seasons in the Divine Calendar, the more I see Proto-Life work in my soul, hence doing my part to realign history?"

His mentor's eyes danced. "You understand over twenty percent, little prophet. Let's return to Adonijah's attempt to steal the throne." Johnny put a hand on Leo's arm. "Little prophet, God just used you to redirect the course of history."

Leo stopped writing. "What? How?"

"If Adonijah had seized the throne after King David's death, his rule would delay God's plan to build the temple in Jerusalem. But, God had someone in mind . . ."

Leo stared. "No. That can't be true. I'm not qualified."

"Clearly, your God disagrees with you."

"But I was scared the whole time."

"All God needs is obedience. You responded when He opened your ears to understand Hebrew."

Leo shook his head gently, watching the twinkling candle before him.

"God just proved He sees you as His Chosen Steward."

"But . . . I know nothing. How could God take someone like me to Israel to do such a great thing?"

"Because He is good, and in the future, you can never doubt that God called you."

Leo swallowed and put his Legend canister on his lap, tracing Johnny's engravings with his finger. Did he muster the right type of confidence after all? "What about those heavenly blueprints you talked about in the throne room? You looked at me as if I should remember something."

"Yes—ready for your second training?"

"Already? Well, I . . . is it related to those heavenly plans?"

"I think it is. Your adventure in the City of David happened through my spiritual gift, but God will equip you differently."

"Differently?"

Johnny laughed. "You look so disappointed, little prophet. Don't worry. I have a feeling the Lord will give you more chances to piggyback me. Come, let us return to the prayer bench."

They knelt in front of the flickering candles beneath the window, and the hermit opened the two Bibles. "Ready?"

"Going to leave me alone again?"

"Your gift is rare. Wait and see."

Leo closed his eyes. "God," he said silently. "I still don't understand how I'm fit to be Your Chosen Steward. But if You just sent me to save the temple in Jerusalem, then . . ." Leo nodded at Johnny. "Think I'm ready."

"Open your hands and I'll pray. Our Heavenly Father. I bring before You my son, Leo, whom You've chosen as a servant of Christ and a steward of Your mysteries. Moreover it is required in stewards that one be found faithful. I pray, as Your most insignificant servant, that You anoint Leo with the spiritual gift he needs to unlock your Word and impart the Life of Christ to key souls. I present Leo Avens before You, Your beloved son. Receive him. Bless him. Equip him. Anoint him. Enable Your prophet to *see*. In the mighty name of Jesus Christ, we pray. Amen."

"I felt nothing," Leo whispered.

"Good. But believe." Johnny rustled through the Bibles. "Do you remember your verse to receive Proto-Life today?" His mentor pointed at a page. "When Jesus was twelve, His parents searched for Him when the Passover celebration was over. They found Him in the temple. Luke 2:49: 'And He said to them, "Why did you seek Me? Did you not know that I must be about My Father's business?"'"

Leo read the verse. "What do I do?"

"The same as last time. Read it over and over again, but slowly. Search for anything in the verse that gently attracts your attention. Focus on that until you see a hidden meaning between the lines. Soon, you'll mentally see a light. Follow it."

"Okay," Leo whispered, and read silently. "Don't know why, but I'm curious about what 'must be about My Father's business' means? Miracle business?"

"That last phrase also means 'must be in my Father's house.'"

"That's the temple, right?"

Johnny nodded and tapped on the Bible, apparently wanting him to stop talking.

The word *must* felt energized—an intense emotion, a craving perhaps? "Must be" flashed in his mind. That's it. *Mission.* But more than a mission . . . something strongly fused into Jesus' soul. Jesus was zealous for the temple. *He took it personally,* Leo thought, as if God injected the words in his mind.

Something moved, and Leo raised his head from the Holy Book. Golden contours emerged on everything in the cabin, as if he had entered a vivid drawing made with a golden pencil. Brightness engulfed Johnny, and the golden outlines sharpened into the whitest white. As the brightness drew back, clouds appeared, unveiling a night sky. Leo couldn't sense his body, but he was present. His consciousness—or perhaps his spirit—was witnessing a scene taking shape.

Invisibly, he hovered across a moonlit meadow toward an ancient tree. As he moved around the trunk, a kneeling lady in a blue dress and light-blue mantle wept as she watched the sky. She looked slim, maybe in her late thirties, and the silver light rested on her white skin. The breeze played with the blond hair that escaped her white shawl. Tears rolled from her blue eyes like diamonds on her angelic face.

Bethany, Judea, April, AD 27, 1 a.m.
Night and day, Miryam pondered how she could offer God more than just herself, so she pursued what was important to Him. If only she could quench her thirst for ministering to the Lord's

heart. It could be a fellow traveler in need of escape from depression, or an overlooked soul in a village her company journeyed through, or anything else burdening the heart of God—whatever it was—Miryam took it personally. Oh, if only her prayers revealed her Beloved's wounds and how she could care for His pain.

To be a servant was her goal and to worship her lifestyle. Oh, to be alone with her Beloved. She abided in communion with the Lover of Mankind. Her spirit was where He rested His head. Her mind was a sacred space—an undistracted conversation—and her soul, His garden.

Everyone knew that if they couldn't find her, search the local synagogue, climb to the roof of where they lodged for the night, or look for any secluded place. If she had time for herself, even just a spare minute, that was where she spent it. She lived no longer on Earth, but where He was, raptured in His love. The time between her withdrawals was a treasure hunt, seeking to be the answer to someone's prayer and gathering the graces of His Holy Spirit like flowers to offer Him a wedding bouquet at midnight.

A cloud covered the moon as Miryam knelt beneath the olive branches. Sheep bells rang and Miryam lowered her gaze. Passover lambs—the feast in Jerusalem began this week.

She rose from her knees. *Ouch.* With her long fingers on her chest, Miryam closed her eyes and breathed calmly. She whimpered. The chiming from the woolen creatures seemed to throw shards of glass at her heart, and the pain was stronger than before. His time was soon at hand . . .

Someone laughed. She touched the rugged bark and peeked up the slope.

Sheep emerged from an orchard, grazing. Miryam crouched and her heart jumped. Two shepherds strode out from beneath the trees into the tall grass. What would they think of a maiden in their field in the middle of the night? She snapped her mantle from the wind and pressed herself against the fig tree.

"Told me to bring them anyway," one shepherd said.

"They're sick," the other said. "No meat on 'em, lambs. And their legs shiver."

"Told him. But he said they'll go for at least nine denarii."

"Nine!? Wouldn't give that for an ox."

"I know. But Shmuel said the demand this year will raise the dead. And that prophet Yochanan . . . crowds pour in on feast days unlike anything I've seen." The man laughed, tapping the shoulder of the other. "We'll make a fortune, Benyamin, thanks to that fanatic."

"Brother. My cousin, Nathan—long in the business—told me the poor scrape together whatever they have. Some even take a loan, gambling on the approaching Jubilee to solve it if all goes wrong. Nathan said the most rewarding tactic is to press 'em hard. If they want to celebrate, they gotta pay for it."

"Didn't think I'd bring the doves 'cause they look shabby, but listening to you . . . you know what? I have three cages with doves I accidentally hurt. I'll sell them to the advocates for the blind and lame. Heard about 'em?"

"Those young fellas sacrificing on behalf of the handicapped?"

"Pretty smart, eh? The blind and lame will never know how their—"

Miryam blocked her ears and slid to the ground, back against the trunk. Tears pooled in her eyes. How could they?! What did *holy* mean to them?! Didn't they fear God, or consider themselves human?! She shook her head, looking up. "My Love, forgive them. Your House is our pearl, and we're all family. Let them find their own hearts and come to their senses."

The shepherds with their sheep passed thirty feet away, heading farther down. A few lambs spotted her and lifted their pointy ears. "Go on, my dears," Miryam whispered, and they ran ahead.

Holding her breath, she waited until they disappeared into an olive field. Miryam ran toward a road, seemingly not bending a straw. She hurried down the road and drew near Bethany, huddling on the southeastern side of the Mount of Olives. Their inn lay on the outskirts, but before she arrived at the blocky stone building, she stopped. Something silver flapped behind a boulder.

She halted and squinted. Her fluttering heart confirmed what she looked at. Stealthily, she stepped off the road, moved along rows of almond trees, and stopped. Up the hill, a man dressed in a white tunic and an even whiter mantle was kneeling behind the rock.

Miryam folded her hands and closed her eyes. Did she dare approach? The last thing she wanted was to disturb. He arose, arms lowered, and her heart beat as it had when she first saw her Beloved. Miryam swallowed and moved closer. For as long as she could remember, she felt a steady flame in her spirit. Now, with every step, it intensified.

He didn't notice at first, but after moving past some bushes, she stepped on a twig. His face turned. Tall, young, and majestic. His simple but magnificent white garments, silver-blue in the night, waved in the wind. Deep-golden and orderly hair with heavy curls covered the shoulders. Miryam stepped closer and looked up at the ivory face.

"Mother. What brings you out here?"

He offered a firm hand and she stepped over loose stones, but quickly let go, blood rushing to her face. "Yeshua, my Son. Will I trouble You if I go to the temple before sunrise?"

The Lord looked down at her—eyes deep blue like crystal oceans, and his beard as dark-golden rivers. His smile flooded her soul with His tender care. They spoke little with words— what could words convey? A glance into those sapphires was always more than enough.

Miryam took a step back, smiling, and gently nodded to express her utter submission and gratitude. "How about Philipos?" she said. "He's so eager. He'd love to get up early and take me there."

"Philipos is shy too. He won't make a good soldier—yet."

She lowered her gaze to His sandals, regretting her presumptuousness.

"I'll tell him." Yeshua's fingers touched her cheek, and she lifted her face. "But what troubles you, Mother? Why don't you come with the rest of us?"

"I need to talk to Leah before You arrive. She's back serving at the temple." Yeshua's eyes reached deep within her soul, and even though she wanted to shield Him from the heat of her unusual anger, she couldn't close her heart from her Beloved.

A gem formed in the corner of His eyes. "Mother . . . you have to go. But I'll come earlier than planned."

Chapter 8

FURIOUS JESUS

In the predawn hours, Miryam, hymning and carrying a basket, closed a squeaking gate and stepped onto the road. A young man with curly hair and worn garments stood bent beside a saddled donkey. "Make space for this, Philipos," she said, her voice meek yet her carriage dignified.

He rose quickly and raised his eyebrows. "You're early, lady Miryam."

"I baked this for your breakfast. There's a water skin there too."

"You shouldn't have . . ." He received the basket and lifted a cloth, sniffing.

"How could I not?"

He looked at her, grinning. "My stomach's rumbling."

"Good. Shall we leave now?"

Miryam sat sideways and clung to the saddle while Philipos walked up front, holding the rope.

"Why didn't you bring another donkey?"

"It's not that far. And I need bigger muscles anyway."

She smiled and shook her head, as Philipos began an endless monologue about everything from the political climate in Jerusalem to his relatives' views on the Teacher.

The Mount of Olives rose to their left, and the road snaked through Bethphage. A few early risers in the village greeted them, but Miryam, concealing most of her face behind her shawl, left the talking to Philipos.

About a mile ahead, across the Kidron Valley, lay Jerusalem. The temple building's white marble and golden façade reflected the moonlight like a shining diamond. Miryam's heart fluttered at the first glimpse. Because she cherished every word her Son spoke, she knew how deeply He felt ownership over His Father's house. She touched her heart. Something new was stirring in her Son, something she knew He expected her to understand. Only one word could describe it: wrath.

The closer they got to the Gate of Mercy, the more Miryam loosened the linen around her neck. A suffocating darkness held her dearest city hostage.

Philipos turned. "We're early. Might need to wait before they open the gate."

As they made their way down the valley, white lilies seemed to blow the evil clouds away. "Philipos. Can we stop for a moment?"

He helped her down and Miryam ran light-footed into the meadow. An aroma of citrus and vanilla filled the air as she gathered the flowers and returned soundlessly with a bouquet. Saying nothing, she nodded to Philipos, and he assisted her onto the donkey. For the rest of the journey, silence replaced Philipos' commentaries on the Roman occupation.

With the city wall towering above her, Miryam stepped off the donkey, her back sore and her legs trembling.

Her companion argued with a stable owner. She merely looked at him, and Philipos sighed, pulling his hair. "Yes, lady Miryam—what is it?"

"I'll enter by myself. Can you wait here for the others? You've done more than enough—and don't pay this man."

Philipos patted the donkey, nodding toward the overseer. "He's self-admittingly expensive."

"Everything in the city is . . . Philipos—stand your ground. Your Lord needs you, but with strong faith and fervent spirit. Pray until He comes." She left him in silence.

Sunlight lit the watchtowers on the city wall, and as she ascended a stairway, the gate opened. Miryam hurried along the golden-hued limestone and entered the Temple Mount.

The enormous stone square of the Gentile's Courtyard, enclosed with porticoes, evoked memories of Scripture meditation and singing under the stars. Elevated in the center stood the walled inner courts with the temple building rising majestically, a glowing splendor sixteen stories tall.

Inside the inner courtyard, beside the temple, stood the living quarters for the consecrated virgins. Miryam covered her eyes, squinting. On the top floor was the window belonging to the room where she lived for nine years. She hummed a Psalm of Ascent and buried her nose in the flowers—she used to fill her windowsill with lilies.

The temple in Jerusalem evoked awe in every soul—she hoped—being the footrest of God Almighty. However, the Temple Mount's southern colonnade already teemed with life, and not the kind she hoped for. Merchants and cattle poured in. Some hauled cages of birds, chests, and religious items, while others led flocks of sheep and oxen. People seemed to argue about where to pitch their booths, and some appeared to offer money for the spots closest to the inner courts. It was clear who thought they were in charge of this place.

On previous visits, the markets outside the entrances worried her. Clearly, Pilate had approved their expansion onto the temple grounds. Feathers flapped, and three young men jogged from behind, carrying cages, not even glancing toward the sanctuary.

Miryam had to find her friend from Capernaum who served the consecrated virgins with dressmaking. Embracing the bouquet, she hurried across the yard through the Beautiful Gate and entered the inner courts.

Four soaring lampstands stood in the open square while priests carried jars and firewood from two chambers. The temple towered from within the next court. Lightly, she moved toward the second gate, knowing she could no longer enter the area where the virgins lived. Being a woman, this was the closest she could get to the temple.

Did she dare ask a priest if Leah had already supplied garments or collected the repairs? She walked to a box with a trumpet-shaped receptacle and inserted a coin. Her pulse increased as she remained standing, hoping a priest would ask about her visit.

The first worshippers entered, and some men who seemed to be spying for customers. When would her Son arrive? Was He in Jerusalem already? She touched her heart, feeling her inner flame flicker.

Ten minutes passed before a priest approached, carrying a vase. "I saw you, madam, but it took me a while . . . here you go."

"Oh, for me?" Miryam put her bouquet in the water and bowed. "Has Leah the seamstress been here this morning?"

"She was just here . . ."

Miryam exhaled—the inner flame intensified, dancing irregularly. "Do you—know where she went?"

"You look worried, madam. Can I help you?"

"Perhaps. I'm worried about the merchants." Heat rose through her body, and her cheeks burned. "How do they treat the travelers who come to the feasts? I've heard troubling rumors I need to confirm."

The priest took a step back. "Are you from the governor?"

She shook her head. "I'm a worshipper from Galilee. But my friend, Leah, has a store in the City of David, and she knows well—"

"Gamaliel!" a woman hollered, running into the court. "Where's Gamaliel?!" She tripped in her dress and fell.

"Leah!" Miryam ran to help, brushing off her friend's garments.

"Miryam!" The dressmaker bent and panted. "What are you doing here? Well, of course you're here."

She poured water on her friend's scratched palms and tore a piece of her own shawl, wrapping Leah's hands. "What's happening?"

The pale dressmaker gathered her breath and grabbed her. "Your Son is here. He's furious."

"Where?!"

Leah pointed southward, and Miryam lost her grip, the vase shattering on the pavement. She grasped the lilies and hurried out of the inner courts.

Ahead, between tables and tents, boiled a mayhem of bellowing, bleating, and yelling. Miryam ran as fast as her dress allowed. How dared they exploit the holy temple?! Was there any Jewishness left in them?! Did God's feelings cross their minds at all?! How could the Feast only be an opportunity to exploit and not a sacred moment to encounter God?! What about deepening their consecration?! What did they think the temple was all about?! She groaned, pressing the white flowers to her chest. "My Son, my Son," she whispered, weeping. "I wanted to prepare You . . . but I had to be sure before shattering your tender heart."

Miryam moaned from more than the blaze within her. A sharp pain of something invisibly pierced her—she realized not only the business elite, but the religious establishment would look with rage at her beloved Son. They neither forgive nor forget . . .

She darted into the crowd of merchants, animals, and celebrants from all over the province. Some fled, their eyes wide, while others fumed red.

"Who does he think he is?!" a man said in passing, wearing an adorned robe and a prayer shawl.

Miryam watched her bouquet as she dodged people and loose animals. "My Beloved," she whispered. "I brought Your favorites." She stepped into a trail of coins that a man picked on all fours. He barked abusive words, eyes frenzied, and pushed her aside. Stumbling into a collapsed tent, she sat up, holding her breath as the man disappeared with coins dripping from a hole in his pouch. She touched her stomach as the agony of betrayal flashed from the thunderstorm inside her.

Rushing between overturned tables, she stepped into the shadow of the tall portico. Miryam halted as a scene unfolded. A seething Man in white garments pulled the rope of a tent, causing the booth to collapse over its owners, who were struggling to close their money boxes.

"Yeshua . . ." Miryam whispered, unable to find strength to get His attention. "My Son—Your heart . . . a vehement flame." She threw the lilies into the messy wake of the wrathful Man. "Thank you for sharing Your anger with me."

Apparently, Yeshua's righteous fury blinded Him from noticing His Mother. He tied fringes of ropes along the end of his tent string while glancing at the men trying to escape with their boxes.

Miryam's heart thumped. This was the first time she had seen Her Son so enveloped in His determination—no, His zeal. It seemed nothing would get in His way. Like a lion getting ready for ambush, He gritted His teeth and pulled the knots so tightly the rope emitted dust. Miryam's legs quavered and she dropped to her knees. Strangely, watching Him comforted her. He calmed the flame in her spirit. Yeshua's passion, thundering within herself, was about more than a stone temple—this was about the human heart.

With a low singing voice, Miryam did the only thing she could:

> My Beloved has gone to His garden,
> on the path only He knows.
> Past the angelic cordon,
> from where the River of Life flows.

With a jolt, her Son swung His scourge, and a sharp lash tore a man's garment. The money changer shrieked, dropping onto his stomach, and his treasure chest cracked open, spraying coins across the pavement. The man groaned and wriggled.

> My Beloved has gone to the beds of spices,
> the impulses of a life tried and true.

> My heart searched many paradises,
> now His garden inside I pursue.

Yeshua grabbed the moaning man and hurled him toward the entrance, kicking the money box after him.

"Because zeal for Your house has eaten me up," Miryam whispered with folded hands, "and the reproaches of those who reproach You have fallen on me."

Her Son turned, eyes blazing. Yeshua moved toward an enclosure with oxen and tore the wooden gate off the hinges. He whipped the animals' backs, and the oxen stormed over the owner's tables and into the neighboring stands. A whirl of horns, hooves, and fleshy muscles sent men running for their lives.

> My beloved has gone to feed His flock in the gardens,
> and I alone with Him, wondering.
> He says, "Your love, not toil, causes,
> my River through you satisfy hungering."

Yeshua slung His whip across a tabletop, exploding stacks of coins, and threw one table on top of another. As He poured out another money changer's income, a young man ran up from behind, holding a piece of wood. Yeshua turned, raised His scourge, and the man dropped the wood and fled. The whip twisted around the youth's ankles, shredding his sandals and sending him screaming headlong.

The furious Man pulled the barefooted youth to his feet. "Get your business out of my Father's house!" The pale man wriggled and escaped, but Yeshua lashed after him, ripping his garment to fringes.

Miryam recalled Yeshua's saying as a twelve-year-old. *Why did you seek Me? Did you not know that I must be about My Father's business?* She continued whispering her song.

> My Beloved has gone to gather lilies,
> His favorite ones, white and fragrant.
> My blooming virtues to Him queries:
> Will my wedding bouquet prove I'm consecrated?

The fierce Man moved toward a group stacking cages of doves onto a wagon. Once the men noticed Him, they fled, and Yeshua loaded the remaining cages. He opened them all and slapped the oxen, sending the cargo thundering after the owners with the doves flapping high above the tumult.

"Take these things away!" He hollered with a voice like His whip as He cleared another table. "Do not make My Father's house a house of merchandise!"

> I am my Beloved's, and my Beloved is mine.
> This is my heart's desire, my Beloved replied.
> Not with words, but new covenant's wine,
> He claimed all of me, now forever His bride.

Less than half of the merchants remained around the portico and clearly couldn't pack up quickly enough. Poorly clothed people poured in through the gates and picked coins, and a group of traders attacked with sticks, ripping the coins out of their hands.

Yeshua darted toward the assault, and Miryam followed in the diminishing chaos, taking shelter behind one of the portico's pillars.

Her Son lashed His scourge around the legs of a tradesman and pulled. The screaming man dropped onto his face, turned around, and waved as if begging for mercy. Yeshua lifted His arm, and Miryam covered her eyes at the sound of tearing garments and a squeal. She peeked. The man scrambled to escape her Son's wrath along with the other ambushers.

> My Beloved feeds his flock among the lilies,
> and I have become one with Him.
> Hear all you who seek Him in the cities:
> Leave. He's not there, but deep within.

The outer court looked cleared of merchants, leaving behind only Yeshua's aftermath of debris and broken booth installments. Miryam recognized the men who slowly approached the panting white Flame—her Beloved—as He dropped His whip. Apparently, Philipos and the other disciples had taken refuge beneath the portico. Worshippers from the inner temple courts also gathered, and Miryam drew nearer, hymning the last verse of her song.

> My Beloved has gone to His garden,
> to the beds of spices,
> to feed His flock in the gardens,
> and to gather lilies.
> I am my Beloved's,
> and my Beloved is mine.
> He feeds his flock among the lilies.

A priest stepped closer to the stately Rabbi. "What sign do You show to us, since You do these things?"

The Lord opened His arms wide. "Destroy this temple, and in three days I will raise it up."

"It has taken forty-six years to build this temple, and will You raise it up in three days?"

In Leo's vision, Yeshua sat, and a growing crowd encircled Him as He appeared to be teaching. Miryam, with a hand on her heart, moved closer and sat. As she turned an ear towards Him, a light appeared in the sky. Only Leo seemed to take notice, and a wall of brightness absorbed the horizon, moving toward them.

Golden contours emerged in the far distance, and as the whiteness consumed the Temple Mount and Miryam, only Yeshua remained as a golden, fiery figure. In the far distance, the outline of snaking canyons and steep buttes took shape. The Lord, carrying the whip and sparkling in gold, advanced resolutely forward, but Leo's body remained invisible.

Leo wanted to run away, yet stood frozen. He tried to raise his arms, but his invisible spirit remained quiet in a strange form of obedience.

The Lord encircled the whip above His head, and Leo attempted to scream, but no sound left him. Whatever he tried, his spirit stood immovable in submission or awe. The whip lashed deep into his chest, ripping a fiery gash. He tried to shout to make Yeshua stop, but his voice failed him.

The second blow of Yeshua's whip threw Leo from the prayer bench onto the floor in Johnny's cabin. He grasped his chest. "Burning! I'm burning!"

Johnny's wide-eyed face bent over him.

"Help me, Johnny!" Leo shouted, wriggling and kicking on the floor. "I'm burning! Quench it!"

"Leo! There's no fire!"

"Hurry! The mug! Get it, Johnny!"

His mentor lifted him to his feet. "Look! No flames."

Even though Johnny's blurry hands squeezed his racing suit, two lines blazed deep inside his ribcage. Leo hysterically tapped. Why couldn't Johnny get the water?!

"Leo! Listen! It's not—" Johnny's foggy face mumbled something. "—will survive."

Fine! He had to get the jar himself. Leo twisted and turned, but his legs turned to jelly. "Jesus whi' me. I'm gon' d—"

Colors swirled together and Leo felt the wooden—

Chapter 9

FIRST SYMBOL

Johnny's cabin, Monday, July 27, 2020, 3 a.m.

The two lashes burned within Leo's rib cage as he opened his eyes. He hurled an itchy blanket aside and sat up on a rug. Quickly, Leo unzipped his racing suit, pulled up his t-shirt, and stared. He touched his clammy tanned skin. The invisible scars pulsated, but they stung less than when Jesus' whip first struck.

A flame consuming an untrimmed wick dimly lit Johnny's abode—his spiritual father seemed to be outside.

Leo grabbed the Legend canister placed next to him and twisted the lid off. A red light flooded his face and he turned the cylinder away. Squinting, he unrolled the glowing scroll. Across his soul's chest shone a red cross. From the crimson marks flowed blue light into the shining core of his soul, and the light in his mind radiated with greater clarity. For the first time, stars glinted in his hands and feet.

Quickly, Leo turned over his palms, kicked off his boots, and threw off his socks. He sighed—was he hoping for lasers to beam from his toes? His brother would have loved that.

In the golden ring encircling his soul, the eight symbols remained too hazy to interpret, but something looked different in the scroll's list of explanations. Beneath "Legend," a golden hue highlighted the lowest of the nine blurred symbols.

What should he make of all this, and of the vision of Miryam? He liked his special power more than Johnny's—a hundred times safer to enter a spiritual movie than to be physically transported through time. Not only was he invisibly present, but he experienced everything from the Mother of Jesus' point of view.

Oh, how she loved God. Leo never imagined a person could be so captivated by Jesus. Miryam seemed to have nothing of herself left. She was like Johnny—frightening to be around, yet he felt so loved in their presence. He couldn't wait to tell Johnny what he had witnessed. In Marlo's Bible study group, they had read about Jesus cleansing the temple, but, boy, watching it happening . . .

No one had told him Jesus was this zealous. Leo swallowed, touching his heart. Somehow, he didn't mind the burning sensation now. Even though Jesus looked terrifying on the Temple Mount, he felt Jesus stood on his side, fighting for him. Leo loved Jesus' courage. There must have been more than a hundred merchants, and He chased them all out—and they deserved it!

Leo exhaled and returned the scroll into the wooden canister. God had proved to Leo that he had the right type of confidence, but what about courage?

Sobbing entered through the cabin's cracks and gaps. Carefully, Leo crawled to the window and peeked out. In a ray of moonlight, Johnny knelt in the sand with his arms raised and prayed with a stifled voice. Johnny's body looked like a tight string that could snap at any disturbance.

Leo lowered his head and closed his eyes. Listening to the drowned voice roused his pulse, as if Johnny was pleading with his entire being. His spiritual father prayed in a language similar to those back in the City of David.

Leo crept onto his blanket, feeling so naïve. Wanting to support his mentor, he prayed a few words until—

A hand shook his shoulder. "Leo. Breakfast is ready."

Johnny marched behind the kitchen bench.

Leo sat up, rubbing his eyes. Outside, the dark-blue hue of the sandstone confirmed that the sun still hid below the horizon. "What time is it?"

"A time of war."

Leo cocked his head. "War?"

Johnny placed a steaming bowl and a hand-carved wooden cup of water on the table. "You must be starving and have a lot to share."

He strapped his Legend to his back and took his seat. His stomach rumbled as he smelled the bowl of buttery porridge.

With bags under his eyes, his spiritual father sat heavy-shouldered, managing a weary smile. "You feel attached."

"To my Legend?" Leo blushed. "Oh, I love it. It helps me understand."

Johnny asked him to say grace, and while Leo devoured the most creamy oatmeal he'd ever tasted, he told Johnny everything about Miryam.

"How long do you think your vision lasted?" the hermit asked as he finished the dishes.

"At least a couple of hours."

"Forty-five seconds."

Leo's jaw dropped. "But it was an entire adventure."

"When you enter the realm of the Spirit of God, you enter eternity. Different rules. But more importantly, did you understand the Lord's message?"

He scratched his head. "I'm not so sure . . ."

"In time, you'll learn to receive a message for yourself or for a key soul God sends your way. I can help you in the beginning. Want to know?"

He nodded eagerly, and Johnny returned to the table.

"As the heavenly blueprints directed the construction of Solomon's Temple in Jerusalem, so the Divine Calendar directs the construction of the living temple of man."

Leo raised his eyebrows, and Johnny cleared his throat. "Forgive me for rushing, little prophet. I'll explain."

Johnny's silence prompted Leo to open his journal and click the pen.

"In our first training, King Solomon told us that God gave them heavenly blueprints to build His temple in Jerusalem so the Almighty could be near and defeat their enemies. These plans were based on the temple in Heaven so God could come and fill the earthly temple with heavenly glory.

"In your second training, you heard Yeshua, Jesus, say that if someone destroyed this temple, He would raise it in three days. Jesus spoke about His human body, moving history forward and proclaiming that God would no longer dwell in the temple of marble and gold, but inside the human being. He unveiled the next station of fulfillment on the train of time, when God would build the temple of the human spirit. If the heavenly blueprints constructed the old temple of stone, what constructs the temple of the human being?"

"The Divine Calendar?"

"Spot on, little prophet. The Proto-Life flowing from Jesus through the spiritual seasons of the Divine Calendar builds the inner temple inside you and me. And once the construction is complete—"

"God fills us with His glory?"

"Not only that, but we move history to a new phase. But that's for another day."

Leo wrote as fast as he could and looked up. "We have time, don't we?"

"God wanted to give you a personal message as well. Ready? But I'll be direct with you, Leo. You think you have to be perfect before you can do anything. You perform your job at Volkswagen with excellence, but you've forgotten all the mistakes you made in the service hall as a young boy. Today, in your eyes, you're the perfect man behind the service desk because you immediately pinpoint customers' needs—and you're exceptional at it. However, you learned from your missteps along the way, isn't that right?"

He blushed, rubbing his neck.

"But with your criminal record, how do you feel when people ask you to do something?"

Leo stared and swallowed. A stop sign blinked in his mind, freezing him, whenever people asked him for a favor or to do something new. In the past, he boldly faced challenges, but after being in court, he felt incompetent to do anything.

"My son in Christ, your belief in being incapable engraved the criminal record into your soul, forever ruining your perfect start. You think your entire life lies in ruins."

Looking down, Leo nodded. "But why am I not screaming at you?" He lifted his head.

"Little prophet, for you, all those merchants on the Temple Mount represent your confidence in your own business plans and achievements. You saw how zealously Jesus chased them out. God won't accept self-imposed qualifications from His Chosen Stewards. There are no perfect starts. You *can* have a criminal record *and* be a Chosen Steward."

Leo dried his nose. Slowly, he wrote that last sentence Johnny said and underlined it.

"That's right, Leo. Clear your inner temple of your need for credentials and accept that God chose you. And if He chose you as His Steward, He qualified you. Your God will move you toward perfection, but in His strength—His Proto-Life. You can offer God nothing. Instead, accept everything He offers you and throw the lilies of your love at His feet. That's why the Holy Spirit let you witness that event in Jesus' life."

A tear plopped into Leo's lap. "Why am I so calm?"

"Because God proved to you that you can do the right thing—even with a criminal record—and the cross of Jesus is clearing your old belief from your soul."

Leo dried his cheeks, noticing his mentor's bright face. "Can you see it?"

"I don't have to. His presence is all over you."

"Whose?"

"The Holy Spirit's." Johnny rose and pulled out a messenger bag from the cupboard. "The Spirit of God gave you His ability to see. It's called the Spirit's Eternal Eyewitness."

"Spirit's Eternal Eyewitness . . . ? Is that my spiritual gift?"

Johnny put keys and a pair of gloves into his leather bag. "Think about this. Was there any point in history when the Spirit of God wasn't present?"

Leo shrugged. "Hope the Spirit didn't watch me drive yesterday."

His mentor pointed an oarlock at him. "You should be grateful He did. The Holy Spirit is the eyewitness to everything. There's nothing that has happened or will happen on the train of time that the Holy Spirit didn't witness."

The hermit closed the bag. "Little prophet, the Lord, in His endless love for you, and in His commitment to your call as one of His Chosen Stewards, enabled you to enter the Holy Spirit's eyewitness. When the time has come, the Lord draws your attention to a passage in the Bible to let you experience some of what the Holy Spirit witnessed. After your vision, He gives you a message. Don't you want to praise your Heavenly King for being so gracious?"

He nodded and closed his journal. How could God entrust him with all this? It felt too good to be true—but it was. The glowing cross deep within radiated less heat, and now he loved the feeling—as if Jesus had stamped His approval on him. Does every Christian feel a burning cross in their souls since they wear crosses around their necks? He hoped the sensation never left. Leo had no choice but to accept the undeserved kindness from the God he barely knew.

Leo knelt beside the table, folding his hands. "I do, Johnny. How do I truly worship? Sing a hymn?"

Johnny smiled. "Don't let your mind dictate you all the time, Leo. Express your heart. And I know, right now, you're moving the heart of Jesus."

"Am I?"

His mentor nodded.

Leo closed his eyes. Last time he saw Jesus, He was blazing as a golden man, wielding a whip. Leo wanted to run and hide, but now that memory made him feel safe. All Leo wanted was to bow before Jesus' holy feet. "I love You, Lord Jesus. Thank You for calling me as Your Chosen Steward. Thank You for my Legend. Thanks for giving me the Spirit's Eternal Eyewitness. And thank You for dropping me into Johnny's home. I need his help. I like you, Jesus. Amen." Leo sniffed and got up.

Tears filled Johnny's eyes. "That touched me deeply, little prophet." His mentor cleared his throat, looking up. "Okay . . . such terrible timing, but we don't have a choice."

Leo retightened the Legend strapped across his chest. "No choice but to do what?"

His spiritual father put Leo's journal in his bag and lifted the strap onto his shoulder.

"Do I get it back?"

"Time to go."

"Go where?"

"Home."

"Home?! But I'm not in a rush now, Johnny. Surely, Bikki has delivered the letter to Mom, and my workday doesn't start until lunchtime after my freedom-adventure weekends."

"I know. But we have to get your Polaris fixed."

"But . . . it's okay, Johnny. It's not that important. I need more time with you. You know—more Chosen Steward training." Leo smiled as charmingly as he could.

"Sonny!"

Leo jumped, accidentally kicking the stool over.

"We're leaving. Now. I'll answer the questions unsettling your heart—but on our way."

"Yes, Johnny. What's happening?"

His mentor held the door open. "On our way . . ."

FIRST SYMBOL

As Johnny took the lead on the narrow pathway carved into the arid canyon wall, Leo glanced over his shoulders, mentally noting the entrance to Johnny's home. The purple-blue sky absorbed the stars, canopying the crevice that felt like his second home.

Leo ran a rough rope through his hand as his only security, upheld by rusty iron poles. A creek meandered at the narrow bottom, flowing into San Juan River two miles ahead.

For once, Leo skipped ahead of his mentor, stepped down onto a rock, and offered him his hand.

Johnny pointed at the curly locks of his beard. "See any gray? You haven't seen this mountain goat in action." While holding his bag, Johnny bounced off the siltstone next to Leo and twirled past him.

Leo slammed his thigh. "Man! Gotta beat you in something."

"Not out here you won't." Johnny tapped Leo's shoulder and walked up front—again.

"I should find your cabin easily. My sense of direction is exceptional."

Johnny turned. "Right . . . did you say your Legend listed nine symbols, not eight?" Leo nodded, and Johnny abruptly looked toward the neighboring canyons.

"What did you see?"

His mentor looked at him, clearly in deep thought. "Open your Legend."

Leo slid the strap over his shoulder and brought out the scroll. "Wow—how did you know?" The cross in his soul's chest had turned blue and merged with the central glow, and the lights in his mind, hands, and feet had brightened. In the list of descriptions, the bottom symbol shone clearly: a golden circle encompassing a cabin and juniper tree inside of a mountain.

Golden text emerged beside the symbol and Leo lifted the papyrus up close. *They wandered about in sheepskins and goatskins, being destitute, afflicted, tormented—of whom the world was not worthy. They wandered in deserts and mountains, in dens and caves of the earth. And all these, having obtained a good testimony through faith, did not receive the promise, God having provided something better for us, that they should not be made perfect apart from us.*

"Remember, little prophet, tell *no one* what you see in your scroll. You're looking at your soul, your eternal self. What the Legend shows is between you and God. But I can feel you're accepting the work of the cross, and I believe what you see confirms that. Only tell me if there's any change in the list of symbols."

Leo nodded obediently. "The first symbol shines clearly. It's a symbol of your home, Johnny. Think there's a Bible verse next to it—kinda about you."

His mentor stepped back. "Really?!" Johnny lifted his face. "I praise you, Jesus. And I was so worried . . . how sweet of You, Lord." He looked at Leo. "The Legend on the Kingdom Map normally shows those eight symbols blurred in the golden circle around your soul. But yours lists a ninth. Your first symbol will bring you to me."

"What do you mean? I guarantee I'll remember how to get up to you—or down."

Johnny beamed for the first time this morning. "Just know this, little prophet. The closer I am, the brighter this crevice-dweller symbol glows."

Leo wasn't sure if he liked it. "Okay . . . I'll keep an eye on you then."

His mentor laughed. "And I'll return the favor." Clearly, Johnny felt Leo's hesitation and reached out his hand. "Leo Avens, my name is Johnny Jordan. I'm your spiritual father. Do you fear you won't see me again?"

"Of course I fear that!" Leo clasped his hand. "Promise me you'll never leave me, Johnny. Promise me."

"As long as the Lord wills, I'm yours."

Leo embraced Johnny in his stiff leather cloak, still diffusing a flowery scent. "Can I call you JJ?"

"Johnny is fine." His mentor jerked his head away, put a hand to his brow, and gazed toward the canyon ridges.

"What is it!?" The first sunbeams painted the top of the mesas. Everything was quiet.

"Let's go, Leo. We'll soon be halfway to the river."

He hurried after his mentor, sweating to keep up. "As I told you," Johnny shouted, shooting him a glance, "those eight symbols unlock the mysteries of the eight Seasons of Salvation in the Divine Calendar. God unveils them when He has a mission for you, Mr. Chosen Steward, during those seasons."

"When's the first season?"

"September, about one month from now."

"Think God will send me on an operation?"

"When you're ready, God will draw your attention to a Bible passage, and His finger will carry your tender spirit to witness something that conveys a message."

"God's finger? What does it look like?"

"Little prophet . . ." The path rose steeply, and Johnny climbed. At the top he froze, as if spotting something farther down the San Juan River. "Remember, our gifts are different . . ."

Leo looked up at him. "Something's been bothering you all morning."

"I praise the Lord you don't need to worry." The hermit, fully present again, reached out a hand, but Leo sprang up. "Now tell me," Johnny said, "you said your father left when you were young."

"Yeah. Dionisio, my dad, is Italian. After Mom married him, they moved to Italy. I was born over there, but when I was two, Mom took me with her back to the US. She was pregnant with my brother."

"And your dad didn't move with you?"

Leo scratched his neck. "Well . . . all my life, Mom told me not to ask 'Daddy-questions.' But I had a period as a boy when I peppered her. Mom moved to Arizona because Dad was not a good man, she said. When I asked why, Mom always said Dad loved us in the beginning, but we moved from Italy because he didn't love us anymore."

Johnny sighed. "Sorry to hear that."

Leo kicked a small rock, watching it bounce down the hill. He shuffled his hands into his pockets and shrugged. "Yeah . . . me to."

The morning breeze blew in Leo's hair, and the sun spilled over the horizon. Despite the clear sky, a distant thunder rumbled. Glimpses of the twisting San Juan River between faraway canyons caught Leo's attention—what was that? He shielded his eyes and gazed at a ravine about three miles down the river. Was it smoke, or the flapping of fabrics? Only paddling and rafting suited this part of the river. "Are those paragliders, Johnny?"

His mentor stared at him, his face turning pale. "Don't tell me you can see them."

"I don't know who *them* is, but over there, something just passed on the river."

FIRST SYMBOL

Johnny walked up close, his golden-brown eyes flaring, staring through him, and Leo stepped back. "What did you see, Leo?"

"Something like sails moving on the river, but it's gone now."

"But sailing is common here . . ."

Leo shook his head, heart pounding.

Johnny reached toward the sky. "Too early, Lord! He's young."

"What's going on, Johnny?! You're scaring me!"

His mentor grabbed him and moved faster on the trail. "If you compare the first time you saw your soul to how it looks now, has the blue light increased and spread to other parts of your inner man?"

Leo jogged to stay close. "Well, during the past few hours, the light—"

Johnny turned toward him, eyes blazing. "Never, Leo! Tell no one what you see!"

"I'm so sorry, Johnny," Leo said, hands trembling. "Sorry!"

"I'm protective of you, little prophet, and I'll never forgive myself if . . . Remember I told you God uses Chosen Stewards to lead history forward?"

Leo dried his eyes with his sleeves, nodding.

"I have to tell you about the upcoming phase of history."

"Okay. Now?"

"Right now!" Johnny ran ahead.

Leo swallowed and tried to keep up. *Just listen.* His spiritual father repeatedly looked back and Leo maintained his pace. This time, when Johnny offered a hand, he grabbed it.

"In our first adventure," Johnny said, breathing heavily, "the center of God's Kingdom was Solomon's Temple. Later on, God filled this temple with His glory.

"In the second adventure you saw Jesus, the Man with the Proto-Life, and the first man filled with the glory of God after evil flooded the world. Jesus came as the first channel to send Heaven's glory to earth—the first Heavenly Man.

"Therefore, Jesus is our heavenly blueprint to build God's Kingdom in our own soul so God can fill us with Heaven's glory. Why was Jesus so zealous about the temple? Because He's passionate about raising up heavenly men like Himself. Watch and study what's happening in your Legend, little prophet, because the Proto-Life transforms you into a heavenly man."

Leo halted. "A heavenly man—me?!"

Johnny tapped his chest and waved him on. "Welcome to the family. That's why the first symbol guides you to me. God is preparing to invade the earth with the glory of Heaven, and the channels are the heavenly men—the Chosen Stewards, together with those souls He's calling us to restore. Remember I talked about realigning souls to their heavenly story?

"In our generation, God needs His Chosen Stewards to realign the flow of history into the next phase: The Generation of the Heavenly Men. Do you want to be one of them, Leo?"

"I do!" Leo clasped a hand over his mouth. The words left him before he could think over it more.

His mentor paused and pointed at some cottonwood trees. One hundred feet ahead, an inflatable motorboat lay chained to a trunk, and behind it flowed the San Juan River.

Leo stood bent, resting on his knees. "But what has heavenly men to do with what I saw up there?" Rumbling echoed between the canyon walls and Leo raised himself. "You hear that?!"

His mentor grabbed his wrist. "Help me carry."

They ran to the trees and Johnny searched his bag. "As you grow in your call, you'll learn to see everything that happens to you through the lens of Jesus' own life. That unleashes Proto-Life into your circumstances." Johnny released the padlock.

Sharp rumbling, like a landslide, boomed from around a curve farther down the river. Leo stared at Johnny, but he clearly ignored it. They lifted the boat and moved through the vegetation.

"Instead of letting your circumstances crush you," Johnny continued, "the Proto-Life strengthens you to be transformed through them. Still want to become a heavenly man, Leo?" They dropped the raft into greenish water and Johnny waved. "Hop in!"

Leo crawled onto the front bench as the hermit pushed them into the current and jumped onboard. "Johnny, talk to me!" Leo ducked at the sound of a blast thundering from the river's bend.

His mentor struggled to tilt the motor and hit the lever. "Engines are only allowed in emergencies here." The propeller splashed into the water, and he pulled the starter coil.

Leo covered his ears. "Where are we going?!"

"To your Polaris!"

"But isn't this a tremendous detour?"

"It's the only way back to the highland without climbing gear."

The boat swayed into the middle of the river and drove upstream between steep canyon walls. Leo gasped. Above Johnny's shoulder, from behind the river's curve, sailed an ancient shadowy ship with three tall masts. Its sheer size hurled waves, drowning the riverbanks. Smoke ascended from the ghastly vessel as if fire consumed it, yet no flames blazed. Rows of steel oars splashed on the riverbanks, turning the ship and throwing rocks like catapults.

Chapter 10

THE RACE: FIRST LAP

Leo grabbed the safety rope as Johnny cranked the motor handle, sending the boat skittering up the river. Convinced he was hallucinating, Leo stared at the ship pursuing them that looked like it had sailed out of a nightmare.

His mentor secured his messenger bag between his feet and glanced toward the vessel. "Get down, Leo!"

Johnny ducked as a shadowy line swooshed, striking Leo's shoulder. He slid onto the hard floor. A smoldering arrow lodged in his shoulder, shedding ashes. Leo grasped at the embers, but they evaded his fingers like tendrils of smoke. "Johnny, I'm hit!"

"It's not physical!" His mentor signaled for him to stay low and steered toward the next bend.

As the ship turned, the metal oars struck a pile of rocks, sending stone projectiles splashing around them.

Leo frantically blew on the glowing arrow to no avail. "Help! Do something, Johnny!" He rolled his shoulder. Was it paralyzed? If only Johnny had warned him about this horror! With his ribs healed, he could have climbed back to the highland from where he had fallen into the crevice. If his mentor had tools to fix his Polaris, surely, he would have basic equipment like ropes, bolts, and carabiners.

As they entered the next bend out of the ship's view, his mentor threw him a Bible. "Little prophet, what frustrates you about me?"

"Frustrates? . . . I'm shot, Johnny!" *And you throw me a Bible. Let me steer this bathtub so we can get out of here.*

"You're annoyed I didn't seek your expertise—it's the arrow. Read Proverbs three, verse five."

Rocks hit the canyon wall and came rumbling down as the ship's towering bow appeared. Cloak-clad figures of the same smoky nature as the ship congregated on the stem. "They're coming, Johnny!" Leo turned ahead. Still a minute left until the next curve. "Why can't this joke move faster than—?!"

"Leo! We're going upstream! Read the verse!"

Icy tendrils spread from where the arrow pierced him as he searched the Table of Contents.

Johnny firmly pushed and pulled the motor handle, zigzagging their boat.

Leo spread his legs. "Found it!" He thumbed through the pages, hearing whooshing pass by on his left and right. "Trust in the Lord with all your heart, and lean not on your own understanding."

"Now pray with that verse!"

A gangplank tipped out from the ship's deck, scraping along the flooding rocky bank.

With gritted teeth, Leo folded his hands. "Help me, God. I'm dying. Forgive me. Johnny knows best. I don't trust my climbing skills."

THE RACE: FIRST LAP

A knight on horseback emerged from the ship and rode onto land.

His mentor snapped his fingers. "Don't stop pray—*ahh!*" An arrow struck Johnny's arm. The hermit grabbed a tiny vial from his bag and dripped water onto the arrow, dissolving it. "Little prophet! Finish your prayer!"

Leo squeezed his eyes shut. "Jesus, I don't trust my understanding. Johnny, and You, know how to get us to safety." An inner whirl extinguished Leo's frustration as heat rushed to his shoulder. The arrow vanished in a puff of smoke.

"Well done. Look in your Legend and see what you can learn."

Leo knitted his eyebrows. "Is this the time for a lecture?"

As they sped past a cliff cutting into the river, the knight galloped behind them on the riverside, pulling out a sword.

"Will that hillside block him?"

Johnny glanced over his shoulder, shaking his head. "Little prophet. God answered your request for more Chosen Steward training. He warned me about the Derailers last night, but you shocked me when you said you could see them. Truly, Leo, I thought I would give you this lesson at least five years from now. It seems the Lord urgently needs you to mature."

Leo clasped the safety rope as Johnny sharply changed course, dodging a rain of arrows.

"Jesus' whip, which crucified your need for a perfect start, must have released Proto-Life into you. And your willingness to become part of the Generation of the Heavenly Men has further unleashed your spiritual growth. What you see behind us is our spiritual battle. Ready for your third training?"

"Yes—like I have a choice. Look!"

The knight, instead of slowing before the obstacle, whipped the reins and rode vertically up the ravine. As he reached the top, the cloak-dressed figure drew his bow. Johnny swung the motor handle, Leo closed his eyes, and something brushed his hair.

The ship completed the turn, and the eerie crew stormed onto both riverbanks. Thunder echoed as a volley of rock filled the air, and the knight charged down the vertical drop.

"Look at your Legend!" Johnny navigated their boat directly at the riverside as rocks plunged into the water, splashing onto Leo's legs. At the last moment, his mentor turned their craft to avoid hitting land and hurled a vial at the knight, who stormed toward them with a raised sword. Leo screamed until the horseman dissolved into a twirl of smoke.

Hands shaking, he grabbed the canister and unrolled the scroll as Johnny directed the boat into the next bend, hiding them from view. Couldn't Johnny have thrown him a vial to immediately disintegrate the arrow? Worst timing for a lesson, ever! The Legend revealed red claw marks in the shoulder of Leo's soul, but blue stars streamed from his glowing core into the wound.

"As you can see," Johnny said, his flaring eyes winning Leo's attention, "these spirits are not after your body."

"That's a good thing, isn't it?"

His mentor shook his head. "They want your soul."

The hairs on Leo's arms rose as three knights rode down a mountainside.

"Little prophet, this is a race to reach a crucial point in God's plan. If we arrive first at this specific destination, key souls will realign with their heavenly story, taking their first steps to become heavenly men."

Leo's jaw dropped as a horseman leaped over the river. The horse fell short of the distance, but the knight jumped from the saddle, reached land, and sprinted up a hill. "And if we lose?"

As the ship came into view, Johnny steered the boat into a wide turn. "If we lose, we won't be able to deliver our message to the key souls. Instead, the Derailers will confuse them, delay God's plan, and we fail our task in realigning history. Then we must wait for God to act before we can reach this point again."

"Are these the bandits on the train of time you talked about?"

Johnny nodded. "They steal, kill, and destroy human souls."

"Did you fight the Derailers before I stumbled across your cabin?"

"If the Lord didn't hide my dwelling, how would I survive out here? I battle them in prayer every day."

Leo pointed at the shallow water. "Watch out!"

"I know. It's going to get tough up ahead."

"Going to get tough?!"

"Their weapons strike your inner wounds, stimulating your soul's weaknesses. That's why you must learn to pray with Scriptures. As you can see in your Legend, God's Word heals your shoulder."

Leo bent over the scroll. *Trust in the Lord with all your heart, and lean not on your own understanding.* Light rushed into the cut in his soul. "It's working!" The claw of burning irritation that squeezed his shoulder loosened.

"These spirits want you to sin, because sin numbs your spiritual senses and sends you offtrack, away from your key souls."

Leo secured his Legend. "And who are our key souls?"

"All I know is that I need to get you to your Polaris. May God, in His mercy, reveal to you where the finish line is."

Leo swallowed. "Is this on *me?!*"

"This is your training, little prophet." The river frothed up ahead, and Johnny navigated into the quieter streams closer to land. "God gave you a vision of Jesus cleansing the temple. Now, He's leading you to key souls who need to hear your message."

"But what is my message!? And who are the key souls!?"

"Little prophet. Trust God and pray—pray a lot. Depending on your inner strength, if the evil spirits' weapons overwhelm your soul, you'll pass out. When you wake up, not only will you be in a terrible mood, but you won't remember your message. This training prepares you—"

"Behind you, Johnny! Ghosts on Jet Skis!" Five flapping shadows shot around the corner, wielding lassoes. "Don't they obey any rules of reality?!"

"Well said, little prophet—they are lawless indeed." His mentor brought the boat to a halt.

Leo grabbed the safety line. "What are you doing?! They'll slice us in half!"

The hissing and whining of engines intensified as the boat drifted sideways. Johnny clutched a handful of vials as the water racers threw their lassoes. Their Jet Skis bounced in the current and hovered midair, menacing faces emerging from the hoods. Frayed loops descended as Johnny hurled his vials. Explosions of dissolving cloaks, ropes, and water vehicles erupted, enveloping the boat in a storm of soul-tearing screams and eerie mist. Leo brushed off his chest frantically from an ugly smirk that had passed through him. Glowing ashes whirled all around and disappeared.

Beneath a colossal shadow on the canyon wall, an army of Derailers appeared on both riversides. Johnny directed their boat up river, full throttle.

Breaking a cold sweat, Leo dragged himself up on his bench as they continued around the long bend. The ship gained on them, slowly bringing the vessel on a direct path toward them.

Leo hid his face. What was his message? What did his vision of Miryam actually mean, aside from what Johnny had taught him about terminating his notions of obtaining qualifications to become a Chosen Steward? "Lord, I understand You have to mature me, but . . . I have no messages to share. And for whom? If only You'd given me a cozy chapel or something to think in—"

Thunder echoed from the clashing of rocks as the cliff above received the catapulted loads. The ship's steel oars resembled the legs of a millipede, forcing the vessel onward.

"Are the Derailers real?"

"You've entered the unseen war, Leo. It's been raging for millennia. I never expected the Lord would open your eyes so early to the Kingdom of Darkness. You witness a projection of the battle in the spiritual realm high above. For all we know, hikers might be walking peacefully around us, unaware of this fight, and probably reporting us for speeding."

"So the Derailers can't harm us, right?"

"Didn't the arrow hurt your soul? Make your blood boil a little? Once God allows you to see the spiritual battle, it's your responsibility to act."

The unmounted knight stood on the gorge's ridge, seemingly signaling to the ship.

Johnny balanced their boat between foaming rocks. "Those black creatures are The Vipers."

"You mean demons?"

"But not as you think. They're intelligent. Manipulative. They'll mercilessly abuse your weak spots. And that monstrosity behind us is a Ship of Tarshish. It's an evil principality."

"A prince?"

"A demonic stronghold ruled by a prince. The Ship capture human souls and sails them in the opposite direction of God's will for their lives. They are one of the Chosen Stewards' worst enemies. They focus on one thing: destroying our mission. But remember, their actual presence is high above, in the spiritual realm. Our true battle—our actual race—happens in the invisible. God allows you to see a physical reflection to help you wage this war."

"Is that why you threw me the Bible?"

"From this day forward, you want to read a lot. The truth of Scripture is your sword wielded through prayer. The Ship of Tarshish is a high-ranking angelic power, not a ghost ship. It wants to paralyze you with fear, because anxiety brings you onboard."

"Johnny? Can you see those evil beings as they truly are?"

"Now that—believe me—God won't grant you this early."

Leo pointed toward a hill where metal glinted in the sunrise. "Do you have a vial ready? That knight is heading right at us."

"Do you realize you've faced the Vipers twice since we met?"

Leo stressed with his finger the dusty trail of the approaching warrior.

"For the moment, you see Viper-spirits as haunting figures, but you've encountered their activity all your life. Long ago, they stirred within a Jewish royal the desire for wealth and power. He tried to steal the throne from God's elect, and thereby postpone the building of God's temple and derail history."

Leo recalled Adonijah's carriage and the crown on the man's lap.

"The Vipers stirred a cruel craving for money among the merchants in Jerusalem, derailing the temple feasts from being times of turning to God to making them into a financial burden the people dreaded." Leo shook his head. "The Ships of Tarshish are merchant vessels, sailing the seas of time, unleashing hordes of Viper-spirits to lead human souls astray. The Derailers work toward one goal: To stall the move of history."

"So they can control what's happening in the world?"

Johnny grabbed a vial from his bag. "So they can forever postpone the return of Jesus Christ to our world." He rose and hurled his vial at the wading knight. In a screeching gust, the spirit vanished.

"They hate Chosen Stewards with a passion because we work to usher in the second coming of Jesus. The Kingdom of Darkness knows that once history is ready to receive the Heavenly King, their time has run out."

The ship's bow rose as if climbing a wave and crashed into the river, sending a surge of water towards them. Johnny made the sign of the cross before the ship and seized the motor's handlebar. What seemed like some unseen hand flattened the wave.

Leo raised his eyebrows, gaping. "What did you just do? What's in those vials?"

His mentor clearly struggled to find a path between the foaming rocks. "Holy water—the Vipers can't stand the water Jesus has blessed with His touch."

Leo pointed at a rider galloping along the riverbed, holding a javelin.

The torrent pulled them over a rock, scraping the hard floor, and Johnny rocketed the boat into shallow water. Metal chimed and pieces of the motor sprayed into the craft. A spear protruded from the engine with the spearhead embedded into the inflatable tube.

Johnny grabbed the back of Leo's collar and he found himself in the water, wading after his mentor. Behind, rhythmic splattering sounded from the opposite bank. The knight charged into the river, aiming his bow.

"Johnny!" Leo fought to keep balance on the slippery stones. "He's coming!"

His mentor turned and reached into his bag, his face pale.

Leo's foot slid on a pebble. A vibrating snap came from behind. An arrowhead pierced his stomach and Leo stopped breathing, grasping at the smoky wood thrust through him. He dropped to all fours, plunging his head into the roaring river. Thuds shook the ground.

Someone pulled him up into a shrieking whirlwind of medieval armor and horse gear. Johnny held Leo's arm around his shoulder as the smoke cleared.

Leo coughed, still reaching for the glowing arrow. *Why can't Johnny be more alert?*

On the riverbank, his mentor flicked through his Bible, shaking his head. "Be strong, Leo. We have a race to win and a message to give, but for now, focus on just these three things."

Leo stared at the arrow. *Only three things? Like my brain doesn't have enough to process already. You dragged me into this, Mister—*"I'll do my best."

His spiritual father lifted Leo's face, his golden-brown eyes shining. "One: Follow me. Two: Don't let whatever you see scare you. And three: Pray ceaselessly, 'Do all things without complaining and disputing.'"

THE RACE: FIRST LAP

He nodded. *Do all things without complaining and disputing.* But this was all Johnny's fault. Was his mentor trying to brainwash him? *No—do all things without complaining and disputing.*

"Number one, Leo!" Johnny hollered, already on a trail.

Leo darted between trees, forcefully ignoring the rotten shaft in his gut. Should he glance at his Legend? To be sure Johnny's prayer worked effectively? Perhaps he needed another verse? Just a second to—

"Keep up!" Johnny waved from the foot of a path snaking up a hill with a cliff waiting at its peak. A dead-end painted with pretty sunshine—did his mentor know the terrain at all? It would be faster to follow the footpath along the river—*do all things without complaining and disputing.*

After years of rock climbing in the deserts, Leo was in good shape, but now he tasted blood. Johnny appeared to be made of something else—his legs just kept on moving. Leo dried his forehead, panting. Down the river, the ship drew their punctured boat beneath the keel. The vessel rocked and creaked, and Leo stood on eye level with the decaying sails. The horde of sailors, though seemingly less agile than the knights, would reach their path any moment.

"Johnny! Seen the rider?! Should be at least one left!"

His mentor waved from above him on the trail. "Hurry! Remember all three points!"

Right . . . but you have a few of those vials left, don't you? Care enough to give me one? Leo sighed and continued jogging, repeating the prayer in his mind. A fragment of the arrow's tip broke off. "Johnny! Your prayer works!" *And you call that progress? Man, this is gonna take forever.*

Chapter 11

THE RACE: SECOND LAP

Leo grumbled, dragging his feet along. The arrow's tip had dissolved, yet the shaft and feathers—when peeking over his shoulder—remained. Johnny had just told him the holy water wasn't a magic cure to obliterate the projectile. The Proto-Life had to restore his soul from his weaknesses, because the arrow lodged in the imprints of his shortcomings.

"Little prophet, as you learn to love God and follow His Word, the Proto-Life strengthens your soul against sin. Until then, pray the Scriptures to remove the arrow."

Great. Johnny is preaching to my face. Just what I need. Leo reached the top and leaned against a fifty-foot sandstone wall, squinting at the sun. Below, the masts of the ship whistled in the wind, and its sinister crew congregated around the gangways. "Johnny, they cast anchor."

His mentor took hold of a rope ladder. "Unloading cargo."

Leo snorted. "More Jet Skis?"

"It won't make you laugh, that's for sure."

Johnny climbed the first rungs and Leo grabbed the rope after him. Only his repeated prayer interrupted the quarreling in his mind over this race.

Halfway up the wall, knuckles white, Leo glanced between his feet. Falling into that hillside of rocky blades would leave him in ten pieces before he even stopped rolling. How irresponsible. Johnny should know his legs were about to give out. What kind of spiritual father was he? Had he forgotten his trainee was a mortal being?

"Leo . . ." Johnny looked down, smiling. "Do you know I care about you as if you were my own life?"

A hooded figure leaned over the top, a horse's rein in one hand and a sword in the other. Leo stuttered and tried to clear his throat.

"Little prophet, what's grinding in your mind?"

The knight leaned closer, seemingly listening, touching the ladder with his sword.

Leo coughed. Why couldn't he speak?! The prayer had muted more than his responsible reasoning. *You should have trusted your own understanding, you idiot.* He shook his head. "No! Nonsense!"

Johnny knitted his eyebrows. "What nonsense?"

Leo pointed. "Above!" He struck the smoldering arrow protruding from his stomach, desperate to silence the mental warfare.

Johnny's eyes widened and he looked up.

A vial glinted in his mentor's bag and Leo snatched it.

"In the name of Jesus!—" Johnny roared, as Leo's vial hit the knight on the forehead. A whirlwind of fabric and a saddle consumed the Viper-spirit in earsplitting screeches.

Johnny exhaled heavily with a chuckle. "You're the best."

"It's gone!" Leo touched his stomach. "The arrow!"

"I praise you, Jesus, for my spiritual son. You've given me a fighter."

The complaining in Leo's mind diminished as he eagerly climbed after his mentor to the top.

Johnny offered him a hand. "We're in the lead after this first lap. Ready for round two?"

Leo got up and brushed off his racing suit. The narrow desert floor curved between the San Juan River ravine below and the highland a thousand feet above. If his inner GPS served him correctly, his Polaris stood somewhere up there, leaking its last drops of oil. He planted his hands on his hips. "Don't tell me we need to climb that as well."

"Isn't this what you love doing on your weekends?"

"Yeah. But while wearing my gear, and without phantoms on my heels trying to slay my soul."

A roar of engines echoed from the river and Leo peeked over the edge. The Vipers moved in procession along the riverbank—and fast.

Leo shot his hands to his head. "And now they're on wheels?!"

His mentor already ran across a country road toward the base of the towering plateau.

"We *cannot* climb that without equipment!" Leo hollered, sprinting after him.

"You know by now this is my home! I know how to get around!"

"C'mon, Johnny! I'll look like a pincushion by the time you drag me up." The hermit disappeared between some boulders and Leo slammed his thigh. Was this a normal day for a Chosen Steward?

Darting between tall rocks, Leo skidded to a halt as Johnny swung the door of a rusty shed, sending billows of swirling dust. Leo gasped as the clouds dissipated, unveiling a red side-by-side. "You got a Honda Talon?! . . ."

"Hop in!"

Leo gawked. "Do you know how to drive?!"

The headlights flashed and the engine growled.

He shrugged in surrender and patted the hood. "Nine hundred ninety-nine cc liquid-cooled, four-stroke, parallel-twin engine at your back—a top speed of seventy-five miles per hour."

Johnny, wearing a racing helmet, waved at him out of the driver's seat. "Admire it later."

Leo entered the passenger side and reattached the Legend cylinder across his chest. "That's five slower than my lightning—so you can be the thunder."

"Stay humble."

Leo pointed between the seats. "And instead of a CVT, you got a six-speed dual clutch transmission—"

His mentor pressed a helmet down Leo's head, stamped the pedal, and spun out of the shed.

Sucked to his seat, Leo tightened the harness while they skidded around the boulders. As they entered the dirt road, Johnny turned the rearview mirror. Vipers on ATVs, motorbikes, and dune buggies whipped an ominous cloud.

Johnny placed his bag between them. "We don't have vials for an army," his mentor said from the helmet's earphones. "Speed and wit determine the winner."

Leo gave his thumbs-up. "You sure you don't want me to drive?"

"We'll reach your Polaris in twenty minutes. Focus on your message and on whom to deliver it."

He peeked into his mentor's bag. "You know I only have the New Testament. Can I borrow your Bible?"

Going full speed over a long crest, Leo's stomach churned as he pointed at a sudden drop straight ahead. His mentor drifted around a sharp bend dangerously close to the edge of the ravine.

Leo's head hit the headrest as Johnny continued full blast. "I read the passage about Adonijah, but I can't stop thinking about when Jesus was a boy in the temple—" He groaned as Johnny propelled them through another bend. "Says here that Jesus said to His parents: 'Why did you seek Me? Did you not know that I must be about My Father's business?'" Leo peeked up from the Holy Book. "Johnny, the road is ending!"

"But we're not stopping." As they bounced off the shoulder, flattening shrubs, Johnny twisted the steering wheel and maneuvered between rocks. "I love that road when days are calm, but I've paved a shortcut up to the highland—one that will slow the Derailers."

"Paved?" Leo turned. The Vipers moved like a black snake, filling the tight passageway between the ravine's edge and the plateau Johnny decided the Honda would climb. Two motorbikes chased them faster than the others. Leo had driven on many dangerous tracks, yet this made him nervous. He clung to the grab bar and the Bible as the front rose and pointed toward the blue sky.

Leo continued reading. "Then He went down with them and came to Nazareth, and was subject to them, but His mother kept all these things in her heart—Johnny!"

The Honda rose on its back wheels, only degrees away from tipping backward. "Careful!" Finally, the front wheels came down and dug into the steep hill. "This isn't a Rock Crawler!"

The vehicle spun ahead sideways, triggering a landslide of rocks. "We'll see if the Vipers are senseless enough..."

Leo shook his head at the long-haired, cloak-dressed man in a racing helmet.

"Eleven minutes and we're there. Gained any clarity?"

He closed his eyes and pictured Miryam gliding into the meadow to gather lilies. Her heart overflowed with what was important to her Son. Jesus seemed to occupy her thoughts and guide her every decision continuously. Leo sighed. His own mother was sort of the same, but not out of such pure love. Angelina's love seemed mixed with anxiety. Miryam's love poured out of her with no strings attached, but his mom threw a fishing net after him.

The Honda slid sideways and Leo jerked in his seatbelt, seeing nothing but orange sandstone outside of his window. They leaned against a boulder. Johnny reversed and threw the vehicle into first gear, smashing the pedal. The front hurled around, clouds flying past, and Johnny's side suddenly slammed into the rock. "Let's go this way instead," he said as the Honda leaped forward.

Leo read from the passage again. "Did you not know that I must be about My Father's business?" Could it be? Did God have a message for Angelina, telling her not to worry about him dying every time he left the house, but to care for his new mission instead? His new business as a Christian? As a Chosen Steward? Could it have such an impact that the Derailers wanted to hinder this message from reaching his mother?—

Engines snarled as two bikers dug into the slope's loose soil. Leo reached into Johnny's bag, but his mentor held his wrist.

"Wait." Johnny honked and waved at the two Vipers. "You look sluggish! It's all the years, isn't it?!"

THE RACE: SECOND LAP

Apparently enraged, the slower rider sped up, tipped backwards, and sent his motorbike flying into the other, knocking both of them off. The bikes smashed their way down the hill while the Vipers continued on foot. From their cloaks they pulled out crossbows, and Johnny drove ahead. Arrows clattered against the chassis until the Talon reached the highland.

"Thank you, Lord," Johnny said. "That will keep them busy."

Leo squinted at the plateau stretching into the horizon. "Johnny? You think it's possible God is calling Mom and my brother to be Chosen Stewards?"

His mentor glanced at him while vigorously turning the wheel toward a sandy trail. "Oh. That would be sweet, wouldn't it?"

"The more I think about it, the more I see Mom's obsession with me reflecting Miryam's obsession with Jesus—though in a more selfish way."

Johnny seemed to think or pray. Short trees swooshed past them on the familiar-feeling trail. Leo would never go this fast, but Johnny perfectly calculated the dips and crests as if navigating through wavy seas.

"I haven't thought about your family as Chosen Stewards, but hearing you say it . . ."

G-forces pulled Leo into the seat until his harness caught him during a jump. He smiled—it all felt right. Was this actually what God had planned?

His mentor tapped his knee. "Let's go to Arizona."

Leo recognized the terrain. "There it is!" He pointed at the rock formation where he had hidden from Fred's Jeep. Johnny rolled slowly around the boulder. And there stood his dusty Polaris RZR.

Tears sprung to his eyes. Thankfully, Leo's visor hindered Johnny from noticing. It was just a vehicle—but also so much more. Barely twenty-four hours ago, he was scared to death for running away from an accident he had caused. But he was no longer the same guy. Something had solidified inside him, a newfound strength—a sense of manliness—and the Legend brushing against his suit felt like a trophy of God's love. He did not deserve it, but God had still called him as His Chosen Steward, and His love voluntarily forced Leo to accept this gift.

Johnny removed his helmet, ran out, and ducked under the Polaris. Leo stepped outside, walking a few steps toward his vehicle. He kept his helmet on, sniffing, holding onto his Legend with one hand, then two hands. His feet stopped moving. *Why am I so nervous? C'mon, man.* With the tip of his boot, he made curves in the sand.

"Like I told you, little prophet"—steps approached—"the Holy Spirit watched over you. Only a damaged oil filter." A hand touched Leo's shoulder. Johnny nodded gently, apparently understanding what was going on inside him. "Think of this as heart surgery on your Polaris. A stronger spirit will be behind the steering wheel from this day on. Don't fear your past. Your Heavenly Father has forgotten all about it—why should you cling to it?"

Johnny looked him deeply in the eyes. "Take a moment and let me handle this, okay?" His mentor opened the Honda's trunk box. "We're a couple of minutes ahead of our enemy. And that's not only because of my tricky shortcut—the Vipers love shortcuts—but also because your teachability affects the spiritual realm, making them drag." His mentor carried a bag over and got under the Polaris, waving from underneath. "Not much oil to drain."

THE RACE: SECOND LAP

Leo removed the helmet and blew his hair away. A low rumbling, like a distant earthquake, moved under his feet. He stepped back and peeked around the corner. Nothing but orange sand, desert plants, and a clear sky. "You feel that, Johnny?"

His mentor knelt behind the Polaris' driver seat, arms by the engine. "They always want to make a show. There you go—got the new filter on."

Leo grabbed the oil can, ran to his off-roader, and detached a panel behind the seats. "Drain plug back in?"

"All redeemed."

While filling new oil, the rumbling moved up his vehicle.

"Little prophet, we need to move."

Leo hurried to the bush where he had hidden his helmet and gloves, jumped into the driver's seat, and dug into his pocket. He turned the key. The engine purred like music. He leaned forward, gazing at the morning clouds. "Protect us, Jesus."

All the instruments and gauges looked good, except for one.

Johnny brushed off the hood's logo and gave his thumbs-up.

"The fuel warning will turn on soon. There's a gas station down the highway, but we can make it home without refueling if we drive directly."

The whining of strained engines separated from the deep rumbling.

Johnny reached inside and tightened Leo's seatbelt. "How are your driving skills on rocky surfaces?"

"You're asking me?" Leo put on his helmet.

"I have a plan to win this second lap, but I must be confident in your abilities."

"When I beat you on this rocky terrain, you'll be confident enough."

His mentor knocked on Leo's helmet. "Little prophet . . . humility. But I believe in you. I said the Vipers are intelligent—meaning how they manipulate you into sinning. However, we can take advantage of their headless ruthlessness to circle behind that evil flash flood and get to Moki Dugway."

Johnny pointed along the edge of the highland with its rounded stone and one-thousand-foot drop. "Let's drive as close as we dare. We can brush the bumpy edge nicely if we maintain good speed. Most Vipers will come at a sharp angle and way too fast . . . So, the higher the speed and closer to the edge, the better."

Leo nodded. "If I hadn't seen you dance with your Talon earlier, I'd be nervous. I'll be on your tail."

"Little prophet. It's time for you to lead. I'll follow you."

"Me?! Sure about that?"

Johnny handed him his journal, dropped some vials into his lap, and patted the roll cage. "Let's win."

He secured the items in the glove box, and the Honda's headlights flashed in the mirrors. Smooth, stony ground and rivers of sand, dotted with shrubs, stretched toward a sudden morning sky. Leo gripped the steering and breathed slowly. A drop fell from his brow.

Leo floored the pedal. Pressed back against the seat, he felt united with his old friend. Adjusting his posture to the beats of change between two- and all-wheel drive—as if helping the machinery to gain optimal traction—he flew past forty miles per hour. Finally, this was *his* arena.

As Leo approached the wavy stone formations, he glanced to his side. A gray storm had descended onto the plateau. Leo gasped, looking repeatedly at the hundreds of Vipers on desert vehicles, armed with spears and crossbows.

Black lines zapped past him. Metal sparked and bounced off the stone surface. However, Leo wore both his new and old armor—praying with God's Word and mastering this terrain through the mechanical extension of himself. Yet the open windows made him vulnerable from the sides. He pulled up his New Testament, opened to a random page, and tucked it under his harness, easily accessible.

Johnny followed his trail, flanking him, as Leo entered the rocky edge of the highland. Slowly, Leo crept closer and closer to the bumpy edge. If anyone dared drive further out, the ground would kick him off his seat or spin him out of control.

San Juan River carved the landscape below, and gray sails lurked in a ravine far away. Since this crazy sweep-the-edge plan was Johnny's idea, he sensed courage pumping in his veins.

The wheels hammered over crumbling sheets of rock that in time would break off the edge. He flung out his rear, balancing with counter steering and the throttle, squealing along a groove in the stone.

Less than three hundred feet from his side approached the first Vipers, but Leo's speed pulled the Derailers behind them like a tail. Arrows bounced off the chassis and Leo lowered his head. Behind Johnny, three bikers lost control as they sprung onto the wobbly rock, slammed into the ground, and rolled off the cliff, screeching.

"Yeah!" Leo shook his fist at the smoke twirling down the precipice. He threw the Polaris into a prolonged slide as an ATV came right at him. Leo moaned as an arrow plunged into his ribcage. Tires squealed and Johnny skidded between him and the Viper. Screams and smoke blew all around. His mentor signaled to go faster, and Leo cut through the next curves, rushing far ahead of the army.

He grasped at the otherworldly feathers in his side. How surreal. No pain—but this type of driving consumed all his fuel. And if they slowed down . . . that would be hopeless. Instead of taking any risk, they should cut directly toward the Dugway and stop wasting gasoline.

The Honda honked and winked, and Leo regained focus. The vials! He counted seven. It couldn't hurt to try in such dire circumstances. Leo took one and poured holy water onto his side. The arrow smoldered just as before. He emptied one more, but to no avail.

Leo rocketed through another turn, pulverizing shrubs, and soared onto a long stretch toward the next bend. As he fumbled to get the Bible out, mayhem erupted behind the Talon.

Johnny's advice to accelerate triggered a landslide of ATVs, buggies, and bikes bouncing over the rocks. Smoke billowed off the edge of the highland like a murky waterfall of screams and dissipating off-roaders. The slithering snake dragged itself off the cliff.

The Honda honked next to him, and Johnny pointed toward Moki Dugway.

While riding the sandy terrain, Leo finally found one of the few Scriptures he had underlined. "Be anxious for nothing, but in everything by prayer and supplication, with thanksgiving, let your requests be made known to God; and the peace of God, which surpasses all understanding, will guard your hearts and minds through Christ Jesus"—and as he spoke the name *Jesus*, the arrow disintegrated. His intense worry concerning the fuel lost its grip.

All four wheels lifted off the ground in a surge of joy, and after a bouncy landing, Leo drew his breath. "Freedom!"

THE RACE: SECOND LAP

From the ghastly cloud emerged two dozen survivors on motorbikes and utility task vehicles similar to their own.

Leo squealed onto the paved road, and the Honda followed. Every bone in his body seemed to have been rattled about. He tackled the first U-turn on the winding Dugway, and the Valley of the Gods unfolded before him. At the southern end, Route 163 would take them across the border to Arizona.

He followed a textbook racing line and shot gravel like bullets out of every turn. Leo swallowed and pumped the brakes. This was it. At the end of the slope, he had crashed into Fred's Jeep.

Hairs rose down his back. Skid marks ended in scattered shiny pieces of car paint, and something red lay in the ditch. It couldn't be . . . ? Bad idea or not, Leo stopped and stepped outside. His backpack! He ran to it and unzipped. "No way!" Maps, compass, sunscreen, knife, empty bottles, and . . . Leo lifted out his climbing harness with its dangling carabiners. A black feather fell out and he snatched it. Rubbing the glossy texture between his fingers, he closed his eyes.

"Good for you, Leo!" Johnny waved at him. "Now get back in!"

A choir of engines grumbled high above, snuffing Leo's desire to ask Johnny if Bikki had many friends in the animal kingdom. This time, Leo ran behind to his cargo locker and crammed his gear between his ropes, camping tent, portable stove, and cooler box.

He jumped inside. "Okay . . ." Rolling in first gear, he passed the road marks and the colored flakes. His chest tightened and his mouth felt dry. The sound of the collision echoed in his mind. Leo stood on the brakes. Hyperventilating, his hands shook. The

Honda blinked. "It's okay," Leo whispered, and rested his head on the wheel, calming his breathing. "It's over now."

Leo crawled around the turn, and the Dugway's last U-bend appeared down the road. His mentor drove up beside him. Inside the hermit's helmet, his eyes must have blazed. Leo signaled for him to lead on, but the Honda remained next to him. A peaceful fire embraced his soul, and Leo wished he could study his Legend—his spiritual father evidently prayed for him.

Johnny moved behind, but as they left the last turn, his mentor flew past. Leo went full throttle and the gas lamp lit. The Honda skidded onto a dusty side road and Leo chased after him. Strange—this dirt road was a detour. Johnny's brake lights blinked and they abruptly halted.

The Honda backed up, and Johnny removed his helmet. "Well done, little prophet. We won the second lap. I knew you could overcome your fear from the accident—like you wrote to your mother. Jesus is redeeming your precious self, so tenderly putting you together piece by piece as His prized artwork. The Vipers just lost a venomous set of arrows against you. Little prophet..."

Johnny looked down for a long moment. He nodded gently. Finally, he looked at Leo, his eyes shining through tears. "It's time for your final lap."

"My lap?"

His mentor sighed. "For the last part of your training, you must go on your own."

"No, Johnny. Please..."

"My son in Christ. I know you can cross the finish line—without my help."

Leo shook his head. "I need you."

His mentor pointed to the swirling dust cloud on the main road. "I'll distract them. That gives you a head start. You know these sideroads. Get to Route 163 and win this race."

"Don't leave me, Johnny. You have to meet my family, don't you? Then you can crash at our place for the week. I'll take some days off work."

Johnny dried his eyes. "I can't tell you how proud I am of you, Leo. You've entered my heart, and I will pray for you tirelessly. Remember. Study your Legend. Read your Bible often. Pray. You're a Chosen Steward now. Then you might be ready for your mission in the first season of the Calendar."

"I will tail you, Johnny. You won't get away from me."

"Until the Lord brings us together again, little prophet Leonyx."

"Leonyx? No—you can't do this to me."

His mentor made the sign of the cross. "May Jesus be enthroned." Johnny put his helmet on and spun around.

"Wait!" Leo turned his Polaris after him. "Johnny Jordan!"

The Honda skidded off the road in a long three-hundred-sixty-degree spin, slamming sideways into the Polaris, and knocked Leo off the trail, stalling his engine. He struggled to get his vehicle going while Johnny raced ahead. Finally, Leo stopped trying.

Yellow dust blocked his view, and Leo got out and jumped onto the hood, shielding his eyes. His mentor rocketed across the paved road and continued deeper into the desert. The remaining Vipers roared off the road, hunting Johnny.

Chapter 12

THE RACE: FINAL LAP

The growling of the Viper's engines faded as they chased Johnny into the heat hazed horizon. Leo jumped off the hood and dropped into the driver's seat, leaving the door to squeak in the desert wind. He opened the glove box, wrote a few notes in his journal, and whimpered. Only five vials left. He brushed the dust off the Legend cylinder strapped to his chest. *Leonyx? . . . What's up with that?*

Leo slammed the door and laboriously strapped himself in. The silence turned into an unbearable vacuum. "Please start." He turned the key and the Polaris woke up. Leo put on his helmet and, just as Johnny had told him, continued along the gravel road, the glaring fuel indicator poking him.

"Study your Legend," he whispered. "Read your Bible often. Pray. You're a Chosen Steward now."

After passing a tiny bed-and-breakfast in the middle of nowhere, Leo drove off the road. He sat quietly. Cows chewed on clusters of straw, and the clouds floated so freely.

He opened the door and knelt in the orange sand. "I don't know what to pray, Lord Jesus. Johnny somehow filled my world . . . he really loves me . . . like You have proved You also do."

Leo rubbed his eyes and lifted his face. "I must finish this race. Keep those ghastly maniacs away from me. Help me understand the message I carry, besides telling Mom about Miryam. But I will upset her, won't I? And what about my brother?"

The prayer lifted the sadness away. Nervous to his stomach, he rose to his feet. "Haven't gotten the chance to say it!" Leo shouted toward the sky. "But You've been so good to me!" The cows looked at him, chewing lazily.

He entered the Polaris and unrolled his Legend. Stars streamed from his soul's core into his three scars, and the one on his shoulder appeared to be disappearing soon. The once shining Crevice Dweller symbol had faded to a golden glimmer. "I'll win for us both."

Leo returned the scroll, revved the engine, sending the cows on the run, and returned to the dirt road he knew so well he could drive it in his sleep.

Continuing fast, yet economically, he passed several iconic buttes before entering the pavement of Route 163. After eight miles, he slowed down as he completed a turn. The sight of the San Juan River Bridge made him flick on the turn signal and stop. Leo listened with all his being.

Carefully, he rolled onto the bridge. The green-brown water flowed peacefully. Somewhere down there, he pictured a ghostly captain sailing a now empty ship. He never wanted to see it again—even if it came with the job. Front lights flashed in the mirrors and Leo crossed the bridge.

THE RACE: FINAL LAP

He exhaled as he drove slowly, signaling the car to drive past. The vehicle lingered behind. Leo squinted in the rearview mirror. A Honda Talon! Leo skidded onto the shoulder.

"Johnny!" Leo waved at him to come to his side.

The gray Talon stopped next to him, smoke welling out of the hood. The driver's cloak looked like Johnny's, but shredded, and a hood lay on his shoulders. Locks of his unkempt brown hair and tangled beard blew in the wind. His face resembled his mentor's but thinner, and his eyes hollow. "Little prophet, thank God I found you," he said with Johnny's voice, yet faintly overlapped with a voice sounding—feminine. "Don't panic."

Leo gasped. A brutal-looking sniper rifle stuck out of the trunk box, strapped to the roll cage with fabric that seemed to burn without flames.

"I know I look terrifying. The Vipers overpowered and cursed me. They're coming. I need your help." The man put his gnarled hand on the passenger door, skin pale. "Hop in. I need the blessing of your prayer."

"You're not Johnny," Leo whispered, his voice trembling, moving a hand toward the glove box.

"Wouldn't do that if I were you," the man said. "Holy water might hurt me. Leo, I believe God has equipped the hands of your soul for service, and it seems He wants me to be the first to benefit." The man's skinny fingers opened the Honda's passenger door. "Hurry before the Vipers come."

"Don't believe you," Leo hissed.

"I look like this because of their spiritual attack. I desperately need your prayer." The man waved. "Come."

While moving his foot toward the gas pedal, Leo opened the glove box, and a vial dropped into his hand. Swiftly, he fired, but the vial cracked on the Honda's roll bar, spattering the holy water across the hood.

The man gritted his teeth. "Careful, careful. That won't help me."

Leo stomped the pedal, spinning into the desert, and the Polaris jumped onto the dry bed of a stream. Alhambra Rock glowed orange one mile ahead.

"They're so cruel," Leo said, his voice cracking. Still a twenty-minute drive until Arizona's border, but he would shake him off—only Johnny could beat Leo in a Talon.

Headlights emerged from the dust in the rearview mirror, and Leo steered left to block.

"Little prophet!" the man shouted on Leo's other side. "If I was a Viper!"—the man pointed back at the rifle—"you would have felt a dart in the back of your head by now!" Leo steered closer and launched another vial at him. The man swerved and disappeared into a dune, avoiding the holy water.

Leo squeezed the steering wheel. "Jesus! Is this Johnny or not?!" He turned onto an old trail toward the rock formation and stuffed the three remaining vials in his pocket. *The symbol.* Leo removed the canister's lid as it honked from behind. Another engine hummed and the Polaris shook, jolting Leo.

The Honda crept up on his side. "Little prophet! At least, give me a chance to prove myself! The Vipers are on our heels and I need you to lay your hand on me and pray for restoration! I'm feeling so weak!"

Leo pulled up a vial and flung it at the man, hitting him. He roared and spun off the road. "Don't like Jesus-water, do you?!" He opened the scroll on his lap and blue light illumined the cockpit. The blue sphere around his soul had intensified. And just like he thought—the Crevice Dweller symbol shone even weaker. "You creep! Stay away!"

He secured his Legend as the road descended to the foot of Alhambra Rock. Jagged formations pierced the desert, towering to his left. Going full speed along the Rock, he hoped to trick his pursuer by heading the opposite way on the other side.

At the end of the rock formation, he sped down the back side. Halfway down, the Honda reappeared, crawling around the corner in front of him. "No!" He stood on the brakes as the man limped out of his vehicle. Leo continued slowly in a long half circle around him.

The mysterious man cupped his hands to his mouth. "Please, Leo! I won't harm you!"

Leo grabbed his second to last vial.

"I look like one of them because the Vipers tried to possess me!" The man limped along, halfway between Leo and the Honda. "Ask me a question only I would know."

"What's the name of my sister?"

The man shook his head. "Smart—I see I've trained you well. You don't have a sister."

Leo stopped the Polaris, leaving it idling. *How? Are they already spying on my family?* "Okay . . . and my father?"

"That one is easy. Dionisio."

Leo clenched his fist. *It can't be him.* How could that man be Johnny when the symbol had faded? Unless—the curse also affected his Legend. "How can my prayer possibly help you?! You know I'm only a baby Christian."

"Not anymore, Chosen Steward of God Almighty."

His heart hammered. Leo could spin the Polaris away in a second, and the man appeared to be injured. It would take the disturbing guy half a minute to reach his rifle.

The man took a few steps closer, arms outstretched, and the wind flapped his frayed garments.

Leo rolled the vial in his hand. "I'll pray for you, but stay where you are. Come any closer and I'm gone."

The man waved his hands disarmingly. "Okay, okay. Let's do that. Pray that the Lord may heal my soul."

What kind of demon would ask for prayer? Leo folded his hands but kept his eyes open. "Lord Jesus Christ. I pray for Your mercy on this man. You know all about him. Please heal him from the curse. Amen."

The man bent forward, coughing smoke, as mist crept along the ground from the Honda. The feminine voice grumbled in a strange language, and Leo backed up.

"It's all right, Leo!" The struggling man lifted a hand. "It's because of the spiritual battle above us." He straightened himself and exhaled. "That was a sweet prayer, but your anointing clearly transfers through touch."

Leo stopped reversing. *My anointing? What does that mean?*

"Don't you remember what I taught you?"

He grabbed his journal. "You said nothing about anointing."

The man bent forward, coughing smoke. "Forgive me. I thought I did—this is getting to my head. Really? I didn't tell you about the Steward's anointing?"

Leo shook his head, flipping through the handwritten pages and scanning the underlined words.

The smoky man straightened up, hitting his chest. "It's the heavenly anointing that gives our messages power. Without it, our words fall flat to the ground. Believe me, people will shrug, scratch their heads, or just laugh at you. If you don't have the anointing, your message will fail. We lose and the Vipers win."

Leo closed his journal. Why hadn't Johnny said anything about this? But he wasn't able to record every single word either. "And how do I get my anointing?"

"Excellent question. It comes through faith, your consecration to your call, and God's timing. I will teach you more about this when we have time—Leo . . . I just realized. That must be why God allowed them to curse me—to test your anointing." He reached out a hand, beckoning.

Leo stood frozen. His mind told him to go ahead, but his heart seemed to scream at him.

The man looked back over his shoulder at dark dots moving over distant hills. "Time is running out."

Leo hit the steering wheel. "Why didn't you talk to me about this earlier if the anointing was so important?!"

The man pointed toward the distant humming. "They ambushed us. We could barely catch our breath."

"And if my hands-on prayer doesn't work, what then?"

"Then I'll pray for you to receive your anointing. Don't continue before you are certain the receiver will understand your message. For whatever is not from faith is sin."

Leo gritted his teeth and closed his eyes.

In a flash, Leo recalled his mental battle while climbing the rope ladder below Johnny. His mentor looked down at him with a face overflowing with love, then deep worry. Above them, the knight raised his sword to cut the rope. Johnny clearly realized what was happening, looked up, and Leo snatched the vial. His mentor roared: "In the name of Jesus!—" And the vial struck the knight's forehead—

Leo unbuckled the harness, his gaze fixed on the bony man in ashy clothes. Leaving the engine running, he stepped outside. "One last question."

The man exhaled. "Please be brief."

Leo took a deep breath and pointed at him. "In the name of Jesus, what is your name?!"

The man's eyes widened and he dropped to his knees. "Shiva!" the female voice roared as the man fell on all fours, spewing smoke.

"That was what my heart told me!" Leo yelled, throwing the vial at the man's back. The writhing man stuttered something as Leo jumped into the Polaris.

"Leo Avens! It's not like you think!" The voice resembled Johnny's. "Don't leave me!"

In the rearview mirror, sand showered the man as Leo went full speed toward Arizona's border.

"Don't!" the kneeling man shouted. "Don't fail your first—"

If that man had told the truth about one thing, it was about the Vipers. Apparently, the remaining Derailers that had chased Johnny were now coming after him—no more than two minutes behind. "Oh, Lord! For the rest of my life, keep every Talon far away from me, except Johnny's."

His engine sputtered, losing power. "No, no, no!" The needle of the fuel gauge pressed against Empty. The gas station was nearby, but there was no time. Sudden acceleration pressed him into the seat and he exhaled.

Finally, he reentered the highway. The engine misfired and the speedometer dropped past sixty, fifty, forty . . . Rubber shrieked as the Vipers entered the pavement in a blue cloud, far behind.

"C'mon!" Leo bounced in his seat. After a series of bursts, the Polaris pulled him up to fifty. There was no chance he would make the remaining twenty-five miles to his home. The lonely Gump's Gas at the end of the straight was his only option. He would jump out, pour in a gallon, and spin off like a thief. Later in the week, he would return and pay—if he didn't suffer trauma or memory loss from a hundred arrows piercing his soul.

THE RACE: FINAL LAP

Another misfire. He slowed again until only a series of thrusts shuffled him onwards. Leo rolled into the station, sweat running down his face. He jumped out, pounded the menu, and entered a car wash offer. "No! Not now!"

Three Vipers on motorbikes led a group of UTVs. A passing car, driving peacefully in the opposite direction, passed through the Vipers like air, unaffected.

"Cancel!" Leo yelled. "Yes!" *Select grade and fuel.* The screen cracked as he chose gasoline.

The bikers performed wheelies, aiming their crossbows above their raised front wheels.

Tears welled in his eyes as Leo shuffled in the nozzle and pressed the handle. *Puff!* Leo jumped and stumbled against the pump as the Vipers vanished. He gaped, the silence deafening. Ashes and smoke drifted past him. A piece of garment wrapped itself around one of his vehicle's bars and dissolved.

Leo stepped onto the road, looking both ways—a roadrunner crossed the street with a lizard in its beak. The Vipers—all gone. A low rumbling drew Leo to squint and shield his eyes. Far behind the hills from where he came, a gray mushroom cloud rolled into the air.

His legs failed. The clouds, the breeze, the mumblings of a distant car radio—everything sounded so peaceful. Leo closed his eyes. "Jesus. If there was a throne before me, that's where I'm kneeling now." He sobbed.

Something flapped in his hair and tapped on the Polaris. Leo got up and wiped his face. A raven jumped around on his roof.

"Bikki!" Leo ran and reached out his arm. "Am I glad to see you?! Where's Johnny?"

"Ki-do-do wing-wing." The bird cocked his head, unwilling to jump to his arm.

"Where's he?"

"Win-win. Kiddo win-win."

Leo stepped back. "What?"

Bikki flew onto another car parked outside a side-building, seemingly a private home. Leo moved around the pump.

The raven bounced onto a Jeep with a dented side. "Kiddo win. Ki-do-do win-win."

Leo approached the Jeep's crumpled company branding and held his breath. *Way To Go! Counseling.* The bird flew off the car and disappeared into the desert.

"Why didn't anyone invite me to this party?!" a man said, as he stepped out of the building. "Bikki & Johnny sounds like a country band I'd—" A tattooed man, wearing a bulging t-shirt depicting a skull, stopped rolling the ends of his well-groomed mustache.

Leo shrunk back and swallowed. "It's just me, Fred."

Chapter 13

ZEAL FOR YOUR HOUSE

Gump's Gas, Utah, Monday, 10:10 a.m.

The tattooed bodybuilder blocked the sun and cracked his knuckles like a predator cornering its prey. "Kiddo! Of all the troubled creatures out there—what's your problem?!"

Leo backed away, waving his hands. "No-no, be m-merciful. I didn't know you . . . don't seek any trouble, sir."

"Looks like you've seen a ghost." Fred glanced over his shoulders. "What do you want? Where are your buddies?"

"Left. Just m-me."

"So why the yelling?! I spilled Momma's coffee all over the table."

"S-so sorry, sir. I broke the screen and can't pay."

"You did what!?" Fred stomped off behind the gas pump. "Punk!" He returned, shaking his head.

Leo's back hit the wall. "I'll pay for everything, sir."

Fred stopped by his Jeep, pointing at the pump. "It's called a *touch* screen, you idiot."

"But at least I didn't run away . . ."

The man snorted. "You're funny too? Didn't expect to bump into me again, did you? Divine justice is cracking down on you."

"But you didn't expect to see me either . . ." Leo whispered.

"What was that?" Fred seemed to examine him. "Your toy is parked over there, so you didn't walk here. Out all night? You look like a mess."

Leo moved his toes in his damp socks, with dried mud coating his boots. He brushed his arms, brown with dust. "Stayed with a friend. Quite a journey to get here."

Fred chuckled. "Clearly. Glad you suffered a bit. But since you did the right thing this time—" The man moved closer and stretched out his hand. "I'm Fred Waylon. Your name?"

"Leo Avens, sir."

"Drop the formalities and move your vehicle over here. You're going nowhere till you've cleaned yourself up and had breakfast with my parents."

Standing before the mirror in the tiny oak-paneled bathroom, Leo stared into the sink to avoid his own reflection while washing his face. Gently, he touched the scar above his left brow and dried himself.

How surreal—how many times had he driven past Gump's Gas? He rarely fueled here because Volkswagen had a deal with a station in Kayenta.

He scrubbed off the worst stains on his white suit, and Fred had even left him a pair of socks that reached to Leo's knees. As he strapped the canister to his back, the pressure to finish his task tickled his stomach. Behind the brusque shell of a man, Leo sensed something soft, but there couldn't be much grace left between them. *I better have this anointing Spooky talked about . . .*

What could he learn from his Legend? Blue light flooded the restroom as he unrolled the scroll. Shimmering drizzle from the blue sphere encircling his soul landed on his upper body. The blue cross in his soul's core made his innermost being shine like a bright star. Of the three wounds, only the red rift in his soul's side remained, glowing dimly. The crimson gap silenced Leo's breathing. *Jesus . . .*

A warm breeze entered the enclosed space, and if Leo didn't know better, he would have thought Johnny was standing outside the door. He closed his eyes and an invisible embrace removed the weight of expectations he had placed on himself. Someone cared for him more than anyone he knew. "Jesus . . ." he whispered. Just mentioning the holy name swirled the wind. "You're—here . . ." Words felt unfitting in His pure presence.

Leo's mind sharpened and he zeroed in on one thing. He was a Chosen Steward with a message. With faint whispers, he recited the verse God used to unlock the vision of Miryam. "And He said to them, 'Why did you seek Me? Did you not know that I must be about My Father's business—in my Father's house?'"

The Legend's window displayed a vibrant vision of the sun beaming ahead and cotton clouds rolling below. The scene rapidly passed through the clouds, and far below lay an ancient walled city. One building on a large square shone like a diamond.

Before the chaos of a collapsing tent and protesting merchants stood Miryam, embracing her bouquet of lilies. Jesus, majestic in His white garments, snatched a rope—the emotions the Son of God expressed quickened Leo's pulse.

The Mother of Jesus threw her flowers toward her Son as He hurled a moneychanger with frayed garments out of the portico, kicking the money box after him. "Because zeal for Your house has eaten me up," Miryam whispered with folded hands.

In a flash, the vision ended. "Zeal for Your house has eaten Me up," Leo whispered, staring at his soul.

He entered a compact living room with retro furniture, colorful pottery, and a symmetrical rug adorning the wall. The buttery aroma of frybread enveloped him. Leo had won the race—God wouldn't abandon him now.

Fred pointed at a chair by a wooden table laden with steaming scrambled eggs and blue corn mush. A chirping canary sat freely in a potted ficus, while Monument Valley decorated the horizon outside.

Not exactly the assembly of saints that Leo had imagined, yet God had made clear that a husky man with an overhanging orange mustache, an elderly man leaning forward on his wooden stick while puffing a pipe, and a grandmotherly figure with a zigzag-patterned apron and tanned face were His key souls. The old woman filled Leo's cup with Navajo tea.

Fred dropped into a recliner next to his father, exhaling a mild hurricane. "Seems like the Almighty tossed you right into the room, Leo."

Leo coughed and put down his cup.

"We've been talking about you all morning and, lo and behold, here you are."

Oh no . . . "Made a good impression, didn't I?"

"You're already improving it. Isn't he Papa?"

The old man touched Fred's chair with his stick. "I felt sorry for that young'un. You scared the livin' daylights outta him."

"Well, he deserved it—didn't you, kiddo?"

Leo cleared his throat. "Yeah."

Fred's mother took her seat at the end of the table. "Is that a plains flute on your back there?" She looked over her glasses. "No Diné could've carved that case."

"You beat me to it, Momma." Fred motioned at the Legend. "What you got?"

Leo scratched his neck. "So . . . I stayed at my friend's house for the night . . . it's just a personal gift."

Momma reached out her hand. "Mind if I try it out there?"

Leo seized the leather belt, shaking his head. "So—actually. I'm here for a reason." Leo sat up in his chair. "So, Fred. First . . . can you forgive me for running away from the accident? I know it was my fault. So irresponsible of me. Forgive me." The sincerity in his own voice took him by surprise.

Fred seemed taken aback. "You came here to ask for forgiveness?"

"More or less." He sweated—what happened to the overflowing confidence he felt in the bathroom? Had it leaked out of him already?

"You were a street-smart, cocky, daredevil twenty-four hours ago. How did your tone change so quickly? I've been around your type a lot."

"Don't know how to say this, Fred . . ." *C'mon, man, jump into it. You got the anointing.* But wasn't he supposed to feel something? "Lord Jesus," Leo prayed silently. "Give me a sign. Is there a green light?"

The big man flexed his arms. "Just spit it out."

Would they scowl at him? Or laugh him out the door?

"We need to talk about the finances," Fred said, looking at his watch, "but you wanted to say something. Honestly, I have no idea how you located me, but since you mustered the guts to come, you've got my attention."

Leo wanted to say Jesus had a message for them, but an unseen hand covered his mouth. *They'll make a laughingstock out of me . . .* Leo knitted his fists, staring at a vase holding red wildflowers. If only he'd turned his brain on, he would have brought his journal.

"How you doin'?" Papa said.

"Yes!" Leo said forcefully, and blushed. "Jesus sent me to tell you a message."

Fred sat up. "Oh, man—you're one of those? Where's your name badge and suit?"

"Of course, the lad had to ask for forgiveness," Momma said, patting Leo's arm. "He's a good Christian. Sweety, that was brave of you there."

Papa exhaled smoke through his nostrils. "Wrong house. We're not open fer God."

"God still chose you." Leo said, looking into his teacup. "So I can't take no for an answer."

Fred leaned back, hands behind his head. "Then get on with it so you can cross us off your list. Just don't tell me if I don't repent, I'll be roasting in the flames."

"Son,"—Momma shook her finger at Fred—"allow the lad to complete his duty."

"Make it brayf," Papa said.

Fred crossed his legs on the footrest. "Fine. The stage is yours, kiddo."

Leo had nothing revolutionary to say. Where were the spiritual fireworks to capture Fred's attention? "I know you will recognize who I'm talking about." Leo flattened the tablecloth. "It's a story about a lady named Miryam. She loved—"

Fred dropped his feet. "What's her last name?"

"Actually, I don't know."

Momma limped toward the two others and sat on her son's footrest, patting his knee.

"Miryam loved Jesus so much His heart was her own." Sentences kept forming as the narrative unfolded within him. "She cared for those around her with selfless love, just like Jesus."

Breaking character, Leo formed a heart with his hands. "The shape of our hearts is a mystery. Not only have we deformed them, but we've forgotten what the original mold looked like. Our hearts don't resemble their Prototype anymore. Do you know Who the Prototype is?" Astonished, like the facial expressions of his three listeners, Leo somehow knew what he was talking about.

Fred's gaze locked onto him as the man leaned forward. "That would be Jesus, wouldn't it?"

"Does our hearts mirror the heart of Jesus?"

"What do you think, Papa? Momma?"

"Miryam knew Jesus' heart," Leo continued, even more animated. "She knew how much He loved His Father's house. She was worried—"

"What house?" Fred interrupted.

Would the scene at the temple in Jerusalem confuse them if he wanted to get across that Jesus was zealous for the temple of their hearts? "The Father's house is the place where God meets with all His children. It used to be a building, but now it's no longer—"

Fred rose, startling Leo. "How did you get this address? This is my parents' home and my name is registered elsewhere." Momma rose, asking her son to calm down.

"Jesus sent me here, and that's all I can say."

Fred rolled his eyes and sat. "Of course Jesus did."

"All I wanted to say is that Miryam knew how our hearts burdened Jesus. One day, she heard a rumor she knew would not only crush Jesus, but enrage Him, so she had to travel to the capital to see if it was true. If it was, Miryam wanted to tell Jesus in advance to lessen his shock."

"She wanted to go through all that just to soften the blow for him there?" Momma said.

"Miryam lived this way. Her world orbited around Jesus, and He always did the will of our Heavenly Father. She demonstrated to us the original shape of our heart, always consumed with our Heavenly Father's business, not our own."

Fred chuckled, shaking his head.

"So often, our preoccupations eat us up. Our plans and ideals press us into a self-made image of ourselves instead of the image of Jesus, our Prototype. Unlike Miryam, we don't know how to cleanse our hearts—our inner temples—from our own business. Our concerns exhaust us, blinding us to the true purpose God wrote for our life, our heavenly story. We think being engaged with our own plans will fulfill us, but our own business actually derails us."

The burly man's throat reddened and a vein bulged, but Leo continued, his voice quavering. "On Miryam's way to the city, she gathered flowers, knowing they were Jesus' favorites. When she arrived, the reality looked worse than the rumor. Rather than celebrating God for His mercy, the inhabitants occupied themselves with their own businesses. But Miryam knew it was too late—she felt in her heart—"

"What was too late?" Fred interrupted. "Speak plainly so—"

Papa cleared his throat and gestured at Leo. "Finish yo' story, son."

Leo nodded. *Does he get anything at all?* "Lord," he said quietly, "is this of any use? I need this anointing. Don't withhold it."

Leo sighed and continued. "Miryam felt in her heart Jesus had already arrived. She ran to the marketplace, only to find Him zealously destroying the citizens' businesses. Jesus wished they had His zeal for His Father's house. Actually, He was zealous for their hearts because Jesus desired to free them from their earthbound restrictions and make them heavenly. He was zealous to give them a heart like His own, so they would live in the fullness of His Father's love and fulfill their true story."

Fred rose and stood before the window, hands in his pockets. "Soon finished, Leo? We need to talk about who's paying what."

Leo closed his eyes. "Jesus—please. Anoint me. Touch him." He folded his hands on the table. "One last thing on my heart, sir."

"Mm-hmm," the man said, still staring at the countryside.

"While Jesus overturned the marketplace, Miryam didn't try to calm, persuade, or stop Him. She remained entirely on Jesus' side, because she—like Him—remained devoted to her Father's business. In her zeal to clear out the market, she could only support Jesus and express her love. Miryam offered her lilies at the feet of Jesus as an act of worship and a symbol of—"

"She did what?!" Fred said, marching toward him.

Leo stretched out his hands. "No-no-no!" He closed his eyes.

Air swept past him as heavy footsteps ascended the staircase, wood creaking. "I've had enough of this! Get his address and show him the door!" A slam rattled a porcelain cupboard.

Papa touched Momma's shoulder. "I'll take care of this, Darlin'."

She grabbed his hand. "Think it's better to leave him there."

The old man shook his head, heading toward the stairs. "This here's exactly why we've been out Sunday drivin'."

Chapter 14

MAN OF RESPONSIBILITY

All Leo picked up from Fred's heated discussion upstairs with his father was "selfish beast." Clearly, Leo had messed up his message. *Oh, if only Johnny were here . . .*

The big man's anger would lead to one thing. Fred would hand in the police report, raw and unfiltered, and enjoy it. Probation Officer Archer would discover the records of Leo's wild escape from the accident and revoke his driver's license—and who knows what else. Even so, Leo would hitchhike to Johnny's crevice if he had to.

Momma touched his shoulder.

"I'm so sorry," Leo whispered.

"Oh, sweety . . ." The elderly woman took her seat across the table, her gray curls and wrinkled, tanned face peering above the vase of red flowers. "I listened to your story there. You don't realize what you've gotten yourself into."

Leo understood that without the anointing, he would wreak havoc. "What should I do? Leave? I can come back next week with roses and another apology—or next month, if that's better."

Momma smiled, drying a tear. "Oh my . . . no, you're fine. But it seems like your god doesn't want to leave this house alone."

"What do you mean? Did anything I said make sense?"

"My husband and I were close to joining your religion three years ago."

"No way." It couldn't be . . . was it possible this old couple—and not Fred—were God's key souls? Perhaps these two would start praying so hard that not only their son would believe in Jesus, but many others as well? Leo imagined a crowded prayer meeting swelling outside.

Momma grabbed a handful of napkins. "My son was a Christian, like you."

Leo gaped. "Fred believed in Jesus?!"

"Oh, yes. And he tried hard to get us to church as well. We joined them sometimes, and we enjoyed the music, but we never went all the way like they did."

"Who's *they*?"

"Long story, sweety. If you don't mind, I want to get you something you need from the convenience store. Think we need to give the two upstairs some time there."

Leo moved the vase from between them. "I have to know your story."

"My son never wanted to see a lily under this roof again."

"Tell me, ma'am. I need to know—if I may ask."

"I fear I'll disappoint you. You're so young and passionate about your religion there. Don't want to take that enthusiasm from you. But—your pleading expression is impossible to resist." Momma poured steaming tea into his cup. "As you may have guessed, I'm a Diné, a native of these lands, while my husband is not. In my culture, Jesus is one of many noble paths to follow. I love his spirit there. Jesus is so pure."

"Jesus is amazing, ma'am. He's so humble—but quite intense when He has to be. Your son doesn't think so anymore, does he?"

"My husband and I were not exemplary parents for Fred and Chad, his brother. We're civilized now, but back when we lived down in Phoenix there, our lives revolved around the weekends. Because then, you know, we could forget about anything and everything. Poor boys, they saw things no kids should see their parents do. By the way, did Fred tell you he's an injury attorney?"

"He sure did."

"He was always a bright kid and did well at school. Sad thing is—" Momma hid her face in her hands. "My husband and I used to make fun of him—oh, my." She rearranged the porcelain on the table. "We were such horrible parents. I can't even tell you."

"But you're pretty sweet now."

"Oh, you there." She rubbed Leo's arm. "When Fred was nineteen, Chad had entangled himself in drug dealing, and despite our threats, he pulled his brother into it. Fred's grades plummeted. Then one day, the police called."

Momma looked toward a faded photo of two boys sharing the same bike. "Chad had gone full speed and wrapped his pickup around a high-voltage pole. The impact caused a blackout in part of town. Later, the forensics told us he was most likely high on cannabis." She sighed, staring at the roof.

"Was it an accident?"

She shook her head. "Drugged driving—they concluded—accidentally hitting the pole. But I've always felt he aimed for it . . . you know, departing with fireworks to get attention. And it worked—it was a wake-up call for Fred.

"Believe it or not, but while the boys were young, we purchased life insurance for both. After Chad died, we told Fred if he wanted to study, we'd pay for rehab and all his college expenses. So off he went. Our son got clean and studied criminal justice there."

"Fred felt indebted to his brother, didn't he?"

"Deep inside—yes. But soon he relapsed. He tried to hide it, but we got access to his grades through his academic advisor there. He had failed exams, and when he realized we knew, he dropped out. Disappointed and angry, we cut all communication. Fred not only betrayed us, but he also squandered the life insurance money from his own deceased brother on what led to Chad's death.

"All this made my husband and I desperate to get out of the house and start over, so we bought this place. The ancestral spirits seemed to welcome us because my brother ran this station before we did."

"But your son is an attorney now . . ."

"For a long time we heard nothing from him until we received a letter with the return address to Arizona State Prison in Florence. When we visited him, he had one year left of his four-year sentence. Fred never told us what he'd done, but we met a different man there. He said a chaplain influenced him much, and Fred wanted to complete his studies once he got out."

"Did he meet Jesus in prison?"

Momma took her time, sipping her tea. "Meet Jesus? Don't think Jesus ever would set his feet in that dirty place. But Fred didn't become a Christian, if that's what you mean. The chaplain awakened his conscience—Fred told us—and he discovered how finite his life was and pulled himself together. He didn't start going to church, but he stayed true to his word.

"Six years later, and for the first time in my life, I was so proud of my son I wept. Fred had passed his bar exam and an accident attorney position awaited in Arizona there. Not only that, but during law school, he met his wife of the Bitter Water people, born for the One Walks Around You clan—a Diné, like myself—and soon she—"

Paintings rattled as a door upstairs slammed. "Just gimme a minute, okay?!" Fred roared. "That kid just ruined everything!"

The hairs rose on Leo's arm. "I should leave," he whispered.

"I won't keep you here, sweety. Can I have your number?"

Muffled voices continued from above—apparently, the conversation resumed through a closed door.

Leo exhaled—after this long journey of finding his spiritual father, receiving his Legend of the Divine Calendar to renew his soul with Proto-Life, saving the temple in Jerusalem, becoming a Chosen Steward, witnessing a message through Miryam of Jesus' zeal for the temple of the heart, saying yes to become part of the Generation of the Heavenly Men, and winning the race against hordes of Derailers to reach Gump's Gas—he had failed to deliver his first message . . .

What would Johnny say? It seemed like what Spooky said about the anointing was brutally accurate. He rested his elbows on the table, hiding his face in his hands, and tried to block out the emotional murmur from the second floor. "Jesus," he said inwardly, "what should I do?"

"You seem close to the spirit of Jesus," Momma said. "Before you leave, can you pray for something?"

Leo still hid his face. "About what?"

"Pray that Fred becomes more willing to take over Gump's Gas. His commitment to counseling youthful offenders sometimes possesses him, and my husband and I worry about the future of our business."

Leo removed his hands. "Ma'am. Absolutely not. You might not be aware, but Fred could experience your love like a fishing net."

Momma raised his eyebrows. "Oh, I don't think so."

"Ma'am. I don't want to hurt your feelings, but Jesus didn't send me here to be nice, but to tell you a message. Instead of entangling your son with feelings of guilt, entrust him to God. Fred belongs to Jesus—like yourself and your husband. Pray to the Son of God and let Him direct your son into the purpose of his life—and I will join you in that prayer. I'm convinced you'll be surprised by how Jesus also takes care of you."

The old woman folded her hands, looking over her glasses.

"Remember, I said our self-made ideals disfigure our hearts. But the heart of Jesus is our Prototype, and Miryam's life proved that God can reshape our heart back to its original form. Why do you think it's so important our hearts become like the heart of Jesus?"

"Oh, sweety. You've progressed far on your virtuous way."

"Because then we desire what Jesus wants. And if we do what Jesus loves, we live our heavenly story, and life becomes what we can't imagine."

Leo's pulse quickened as the words rolled off his tongue. "Jesus' heart churned when He walked on the earth. Those He loved didn't understand Him, the people He came to save persecuted Him, and the leaders who were supposed to prepare the nation for His coming condemned Him to death. But Jesus responded with goodness, because of His love for His Heavenly Father and us all, and instead carried the burden of our unrighteousness toward the cross of His execution. When He lifted the wood onto His scourged back, the joy of a future age shone before Him, and He endured. Do you know what His joy was?"

Momma shook her head, holding a napkin.

"Jesus gazed toward the day of the gladness of His heart, the day of His heavenly wedding."

"Wedding?"

"A spiritual one—not between a man and a woman, but between Himself and us. One day, our entire being will fully unite with Jesus, and glory will shine from His heart, unhindered through ours, and flood the entire world with the knowledge of Him.

Leo leaned forward. "Ma'am, during His incomprehensible suffering, Jesus found His joy in you, in me, in your husband, and in Fred, as He watched with hope into our future that we would be His Bride of human souls. This joy made Him despise the shame of His execution and endure the crucifixion until His death. But Jesus rose from the grave to give us His Life—the original human Life—so God can forgive our wrongs and cultivate our heart into an infinite Paradise of His delight. How do you think we receive this eternal Life?"

"By becoming Christians?"

"Not sure what you mean by Christian, but it's simple. We receive Life by loving Jesus more than anything else. Because loving other things more than Jesus deforms our hearts and derails our lives from our heavenly story, but loving Him reshapes and realigns our hearts to His own."

The stairs creaked. "Darlin', need you."

Momma cleared her throat, looking toward her husband. "Sorry—what? Now?"

"Need to have a lil' chat about the future of this place. Fred is not gonna be takin' charge of the management."

"Is he now? He's fixed on going after those young criminals, isn't he?" Momma glanced at Leo. "To give them a better future . . ."

"Leave young Leo and come on over."

The elderly lady dried her eyes. "Just a moment." She leaned forward and whispered. "Not sure what's going on up there but will you pray for us, honey?"

He nodded eagerly. "Can I pray here?"

Alone, Leo knelt before the window. The never-ending bright sky above the orange desert seemed to invite a conversation. Next to him, the household songbird trilled, and a discussion buzzed from the ceiling.

Leo closed his eyes. "My Lord Jesus, help these parents champion Fred's dream—and help him support his parents. Those two are Your key souls. Help them get to know You." Leo thanked Jesus for sending him there, protecting him, and giving him words that were as new for himself as for his listeners. His prayer returned to Miryam's story and Jesus cleansing the temple.

Losing track of time, Leo recalled his entire vision, from Miryam eavesdropping on the shepherds, to riding the donkey, to the Temple Mount. "Oh, that Papa and Momma heard what they needed to hear. Jesus, You chased out the merchants because of Your zeal for the living temple of man. The traders' actions showed their deformed hearts, but Lord—You whipped me too . . . You're so jealous of Your wedding. Nothing gets between You and Your Bride. You'll tear down our marketplace of lies if we don't see the truths You've revealed."

"Kiddo." Fred filled the doorframe, brows furrowed.

Leo jumped to his feet, blood rushing to his face. "S-sorry, I forgot the time. I'll leave right away."

"Outside." The big man disappeared into the hallway.

Leo hurried to the entrance, and Fred, holding an envelope, opened the door but remained inside. "Step out."

"O-okay." Leo avoided eye contact until a tattooed log of a forearm blocked him.

Fred flexed his jaw. "See this?" He flapped the envelope. "The police report will revoke your license and put you on probation for at least twelve months. Believe me, that's a conservative estimate for what I've documented here, including links to videos. Depending on your criminal record, you might as well end up behind bars."

"Fred. *Please*. I *beg* you. My family's situation . . . if I can't work, our plans for my brother will—"

The man's bulky fists shredded the envelope and shuffled the pieces into Leo's hands. "Bring it to the cross," Fred said, his eyes watery. "I forgive you." The man stormed outside.

The ball of snow-white cellulose silenced the choir of accusing voices around Leo's shoulders and unleashed a sigh from his depths. He stared, moving his fingers. The stinger of anxiety, extracted and overcome in his hands, released a fountain of gratitude. Too good to be true—but it was. "It's over then . . ." he whispered. Leo stuffed the crumpled paper into his pockets as his trophy from winning the race and stepped outside.

Fred leaned against his Jeep with a hand covering his eyes. Gently, Leo walked up to his Polaris across from him.

"I'm guessing you have a few questions." Fred removed his hands from his red face, his eyes swollen.

"Yes, but . . . what you just did . . . don't know what to say."

"You've said enough already." Fred kicked a pebble across the yard, clanging into a rusty oil barrel. "Yesterday, I never would have guessed you were a Christian brother."

"Well, I . . ." Leo leaned against the Polaris, biting his lip—having the same thought.

"How long have you known the Lord?"

Leo rubbed his calf with his foot. "Two months and twenty-seven days."

"I see. That explains a few things. Still a lot of drag from your old life to turn away from, right?"

"Well, I just realized it's part of the process."

"I'll be the last person to preach integrity to your face. Obviously, you don't know what it means to walk away from the Lord in anger, trying to convince yourself and others you've turned your back on Jesus."

Leo shook his head. "You did a pretty good job though."

Fred pulled a hand down his face. "Oh boy. Since yesterday, you don't know what monsoon you have stirred inside me. I don't know why—putting the circumstances aside—but there was something about you that hammered all my buttons, and it bothered me so much I've barely slept. An ambush of all kinds of thoughts rained over me. But this morning . . . you helped me face myself, Leo. I'm a selfish beast. Gotta tell you, it takes God to love someone like me."

A knot tightened in Leo's stomach. "Did anything of what I said make sense to you?"

The man seemed to examine him, and Leo watched a scurrying lizard to evade his probing eyes. "My wife's name was Miriam."

Leo gasped, lifting his face.

"Healing oil to my parched soul . . . she was an angel. So beautiful. A Catholic. Don't want to get into the nitty-gritty, but while I served time, Christianity attracted me, and during law school this woman sealed the deal. You must understand, I still hadn't bowed my heart to Jesus, but on the outside, I pulled myself together enough to be convincing.

"My wife got a job as a family lawyer and we adopted a beautiful girl. Evelyn is fourteen now—she's with her other grandparents today—and when she's old enough, I'm gonna make sure she stays far away from you."

Leo blushed, not knowing where to put his hands. "Oh. No problem. I'm not interested in any relationships."

"I'm kidding, kiddo—almost . . . But the problem with Miriam was that her heart was too big and I was stingy. She got in contact with a Catholic mission, Hands of Jesús, and she went on brief trips to an orphanage in Mexico City as a volunteer. The staff began calling when she was home, and when I answered, they spoke more and more casually—as if they knew me even though I had never met them. It annoyed me because I don't leave my private number, address, or anything leading back to my home with anyone."

"I don't know them," Leo said quickly. "Jesus led me to this station, for real."

Fred sighed. "Guess I owe you an apology too. You've seen my rebellion against God through my enforced, unpolished behavior. Embarrassing—humbling at best. Sorry about all that, kiddo."

Leo tapped his heart and pointed at the Jeep's dented side. "So what am I supposed to say then?"

"Good point. Forgive and forget, shall we?"

He nodded eagerly. "Did you ever travel with your wife to the orphanage?"

"After her trips extended from a long weekend, to a whole week, to several weeks, to her entire vacation, I reluctantly came along—had my reservations about Mexico. But once I came down and saw the work—man, that put things into perspective. Entire families spend their days searching people's garbage for something, anything, they can eat or sell.

"When I watched my wife loving the orphans . . . I realized how sinful I was. I got jealous—can you believe it? Those poor kids, having no parents to care for them—and I felt bitter when Miriam poured out her love. One infant was abandoned at a garbage dump, like some toy. Another on the orphanage's doorstep during a rainstorm at night so we couldn't identify the parents. Imagine leaving your child like that. And then I got sour when my wife took care of them . . ."

"Forgive me if my story condemned you, sir."

"Oh, I knew how wrong my envy was, and I felt it again and again, but I couldn't change my heart. I was utterly helpless. Then, one night at the orphanage, I had a dream. I saw my wife embracing a kid and I ran into my room, ashamed of how I felt. Suddenly, a man in a white robe stood there. He said nothing. Just walked over and hugged me—like my wife did with the orphans—warming my heart until the thing that enclosed it crumbled. I felt so loved. Then I knew Who it was, and I woke up.

"Leo, when I think of how Jesus embraced me—" Fred looked away, his chin quavering. The big man rubbed his face. "Man . . . Leo. Today, I realized it again. When you told your story about Mary and how her life revolved around Jesus—your words seared the rock in my chest. I remembered Jesus deserves that kind of love from us, because of how He—how He loves us. Then I thought about my rebellion for the past two years—man!" Fred hit his Jeep, startling Leo.

"I'm a snotty teenager," Fred continued, lifting his arms toward the sky and shaking his head. "Lord, I'm such a brat!

Forgive me! I'm coming back to You now!" He rested his arms against his sides, looking down.

Once Leo's heartbeat calmed, he broke the silence. "What happened after your dream?"

"I gave my life to the Lord that night. From that day, I became a Christian on the inside—a world of difference. And the first thing I noticed was that my jealousy was gone. Jesus—*amazing* Jesus—did a miracle in my heart. For three years, we lived in Mexico City and took over the management of the orphanage. We cared for forty orphans, all with heart-shredding stories you wouldn't believe if I told you. But three years ago, my worst nightmare became true.

"Miriam lost weight, saying she had no appetite. The doctors couldn't find anything until . . ." Fred moaned. "Until they diagnosed her with stage four pancreatic cancer. The following year became a black hole with flashes of my deteriorating Beauty, the orphans' anxious faces, and torturous calls with insurance companies. My knees ached after weeping my heart out in prayer. I was exhausted, broken—and more and more angry with God."

Fred walked off, waving his arms, seemingly performing breathing exercises.

"You don't have to tell this story when it's so painful, Fred. I see the picture."

"Oh, Leo, you don't know how helpful it is to air this with you." The big man sat down against the Jeep, his arms resting on his knees and head hanging. "Two years ago, I flew my wife's coffin back home to the States. I was done with the orphanage. I was done with church missions. And I was done with Jesus. And that's been my life for the past two years."

Fred lifted a dejected face. "I've received countless emails from Hands of Jesús and the orphanage, but I deleted most. Only skimmed through a few. I've learned enough to know they're in terrible trouble. The guy who stepped in after I left is not the right man. Frankly, many staff and volunteers quit because of him and now he's leaving as well. The last email I read two months ago said their situation would force Hands of Jesús to close the orphanage. That's . . . that's just wrong, no matter how you look at it."

Leo sat on one of the Polaris' wheels. "And there's no one who can take over?"

"Doesn't seem like it. In the meantime, I've been busy with my old passion as an accident attorney and my work with getting kids off the street before they hurt themselves or others." He hit the dented *Way To Go! Counseling* logo on the Jeep's door. "That's been my preoccupation, but today I realized it's been my way to drown God's voice, or to use your language, my business in deforming my heart."

They remained silent until Fred chuckled. "Remember the story in the Old Testament when God made the donkey speak?"

"A speaking donkey . . . ?" Leo scratched his head. "Not so sure I . . ."

"What I want to say—and you probably don't have a clue—is that God used you mightily."

"Really?!" Leo jumped to his feet. "Did He?"

"Don't know how to say this, kiddo, as embarrassing as it is, but this is a turning point in my life."

"Is it?!"

"Do you know the name my wife gave the orphanage?"

"The Heart of Jesus?"

"The Lily."

Leo's jaw dropped.

"I snapped when you said the Mother of Jesus wanted to support her Son's cleansing of the temple by throwing lilies at His feet. God spoke clearly to my heart when you said those words."

Leo grabbed a bar of his roll cage.

"I once betrayed a man very close to me," Fred continued, "and Jesus told me today I'm about to betray my wife the same way.

"Miriam christened the orphanage The Lily because the children were God's lilies and the orphanage was the Heavenly Father's house. She had such a capacity to love them because she loved Jesus tremendously. Her work at The Lily was how she loved God. When we prayed together before going to sleep, Miriam always placed the orphanage at the feet of Jesus so the children would have a peaceful night—like your story when Mary threw her flowers.

"As for that monkey who so quickly grabbed the leadership after I left, well . . . it's time I follow Jesus's example to clear out that house as well. I won't turn my back on The Lily anymore."

Leo wiped his eyes. "Are you going there again?" he whispered.

"I discussed with Papa and Momma while you were downstairs. Even though I love Way To Go! Counseling, I know it's not my calling. I will close my business and move back to The Lily in Mexico City. Also, I remembered today what my wife told me the week before she was diagnosed. She said, 'On the first night I served here, I dreamed about the lilies as teenagers and young adults illuminating Mexico's *pobre, miserable* places with a light from Heaven.' I will not let my wife down, nor her lilies.

"I'll ask Evelyn if she wants to move there, but knowing her, she'll probably only come for visits and live here at the Station. By the way, I'm not sure what you chatted with Momma about, but she was all in when I explained all this. Papa was skeptical—worried about my mental health—but Momma convinced him. Said she wanted to attend Mass on Sundays as well . . ."

"I . . . I don't know what to say, Fred."

"Well, start by praising Jesus, because The Lily's financial problem was my immediate worry when thinking about returning. But suddenly Papa turned on his heels as well. He wanted the profit of Gump's Gas to support me and The Lily. Quite amazing, this whole place will serve God's Kingdom."

Fred got to his feet. "I can't grasp what's going on. Everything is turning on its head. Kiddo, if you hadn't come this morning, the police would be thumbing through my report about you now. I documented the entire story, and I told you what the consequences would be. But, hey!—" Fred opened his arms. "Give this big brother a bear hug, will you?"

Leo approached the outstretched arms, his vision blurred through tears. "Just *remember* I'm made of *bones*!" he said, feet dangling.

Fred let him down. "Don't forget to pray for me, kiddo. You're a man of responsibility, and I trust you and your close relationship with God."

Overwhelmed, Leo shrugged and nodded.

"Also, Papa told me whenever you fill gas here, just tell the cashier your name is Kiddo, and Papa will pay on your behalf."

"Really?!"

"Yup. Gump's Gas serves God now—that includes taking care of you. It's scary to think about, but in the past week, a thought seemed to hit me out of nowhere about offering Way To

Go! Counseling to the State as a government-funded program. I felt convinced I had the experience to offer something that's missing among the rehab programs—and I was sure this was my niche. Even this morning, I decided I would contact SAMHSA after I returned from the police. Good you arrived before I left, huh?"

"You have no idea, Fred."

The sturdy man reached out his hand. "Can't help it, kiddo. But I like you. You'll keep in touch, won't you?"

"Of course I will. Have to know what's happening with you all. I guarantee I'll fuel up here from now on."

"Not sure when I'll see you again. I live down in Phoenix, and I visit the old folks at least every other weekend, but I'm sure the Lord will make our paths cross. You just keep on praying for me, you hear?"

"What about the touch screen I broke?"

"Forget about that." Fred inspected his Polaris. "Better get your license plate on, you thug."

"Yes, sir."

Fred waved and walked inside.

Strapped in his Polaris, Leo couldn't leave Gump's Gas until he had fully absorbed what had happened. The property hosted two gas pumps, a convenience store with a car wash on the side, the Waylon family's simple home, and an ancient Chevrolet Bel Air parked in an abandoned auto repair shop, its radio playing country music. Such an insignificant place in the middle of nowhere—but a shining hub on the Kingdom Map.

The compressed *Way To Go! Counseling* logo on the Jeep drew his attention. "Jesus, forgive me for doubting. He was a key soul after all." As Leo stared, replaying the slow-motion collision with Fred and Papa in his mind, it dawned on him. Not only did God use the accident to chase Leo into Johnny's crevice and realign his life as a Chosen Steward, but God used the crash to release Fred from his business and restore his call to The Lily orphanage. How could God use that single event—seemingly so destructive—to birth a new life for both of them?

Leo flipped through his journal. "Is this what You mean with the Divine Calendar, Jesus? Can everything that happens be a channel to receive Your Proto-Life, if I accept it from Your hand and understand it from what happened to You?" A small whirlwind swept through the yard, chasing a tumbleweed. "Guess so . . ."

Leo turned the key, drove onto the highway, and soon after passed a sign. *Welcome to Arizona.* Apparently, the release of stress churned his stomach and he pulled over. It tickled. Did Momma's tea contain a spell or something? Leo giggled. *Great. I'm going crazy.* He chuckled to himself.

Joy whirled from deep within, surging up like geysers in his throat. With springing tears, Leo covered his mouth until he burst into laughter. *What's going on?!* "Lord! Make it stop!" Impossible. He laughed from his core, and the thought of checking his Legend only loosened more guffaws. *"This—isn't—funny!"* he gasped in between fits.

He surrendered, wriggling in the harness. Anyone with ears hundreds of feet away would have heard him howling with laughter.

Epilogue

NEW BEGINNING

Southwest of Monument Valley, Arizona, Monday, July 27, 2020

The spurts of laughter had finally dried out as Leo turned off Route 163. Beyond several rising hills, a house upon a saffron crest welcomed him. Leo wanted to disarm his mother's ticking anxieties before they exploded in his face, then go to his room, kneel, and unroll his Legend.

On his right towered Agathla Peak, a one-thousand-five-hundred-feet-tall umber pinnacle, surrounded by rugged desert plains. Even from afar, this rock formation—which in his childhood imagination was the petrified hand of a giant standing on the earth's core—made Leo feel safe. *El Capitan, home sweet home.*

He drove past their only neighbors, the Yazzie family. A woman in her late fifties left her porch wearing a flapping shawl, holding onto her spring green sunhat. Supported by her walking stick, she beckoned as she entered the arid yard with three car wrecks.

Leo waved out the window. "Mrs. Yazzie!" She said something indiscernible. "Can't hear you, Nana-Mai," he continued, "but have a joyful day!" She pointed at her ear and shrugged. "Love you too!" Mrs. Yazzie laughed and waved him off, returning to her shade.

Finally, he reached a tattered wooden gate and jumped out. He shielded his eyes, taken aback by the rushing clouds against the clear blue, camouflaging the vast landscape with charcoal shades. What a painting!

Gusts rippled the grass on the ten-acre lot, rattled a bucket hanging above an old well, and swirled brass-colored dust over patches of golden sand. A weathered but tidy chestnut house with a slender veranda and a second floor added to half the building stood distinguished. An old shed with a silver metallic sheen glinted at the far end of the land.

Leo drove into the carport and parked next to his mother's donated and strikingly yellow Kia Soul. Leaning his head against the headrest, he sighed. He grabbed his journal and the last holy water vial from the glove locker and headed around to the cargo case. Hastily, Leo unstrapped his Legend and hid it in his climbing-gear rucksack. He left his camping tent, portable stove, and cooler box for later, flung the backpack on his shoulder, and walked along the backside of his house.

A piece of wood tapped against the bottom of the siding, and Leo moved closer and kicked. "Nailed it." He entered the front yard where the wind whispered in a juniper tree.

"Leo!" A slim woman with a flowery headscarf, brown dreadlocks, and a denim jacket ran out of the house.

"Hey Mom."

"My Leo!" Angelina threw her arms around his neck and kissed his cheek, smelling of her usual lavender. "What took you so long?!"

EPILOGUE: NEW BEGINNING

"Ran out of gas."

She grabbed his racing jacket and shook him. "I want to kill you! Why didn't you borrow someone's phone?!"

Leo seized her hands. "Stop it! Mom, I've been in the desert—you don't read smoke signals."

A few inches shorter, his mother snatched back her hands and held onto Leo's shoulders, mascara streaking down her face. "I've been so anxious I'm nauseous. How did he treat you?!"

"Who?"

From her pocket, Angelina grabbed a roll of yellow paper and slapped his head. "Johnny!" she said. "Was about to google his name and track you down."

He stared until he recalled Bikki's mail delivery. "I see. Yes—googling Johnny would have definitely located him right away."

She hit his shoulder with his letter. "Are you hungry?! You've been crying, haven't you?"

He dried his eyes. "Must be the wind."

"Tell me the truth!"

"Hey, calm down, Mom. I'm here now, perfectly fine."

She struck him again. "Then why does your hair look like a dust devil?!"

Leo reached out his hand. "Can I have that?"

Angelina smacked the paper into his hand, scattering wax remnants, and crossed her arms. "Have you been drinking?"

Leo gaped. "What?! What makes you think that?" She bent forward and sniffed, and he recoiled. "Mom, I have not!"

"Then why are you so smiley? You're beaming."

He grabbed his hair, laughing. "Just because I'm happy you think I've been drinking? Well, you should know I don't do any of those things anymore."

She sighed. "Swear you didn't."

"You must believe me, Mom. Not for six months—exactly."

Angelina pursed her lips, shook her head, and embraced him again. "I've been imagining all kinds of things that could have—"

"I know you have. That's why I wrote, so you—"

"How much will this cost us? I'm reminding you, young man, that I didn't get the raise."

Leo waved the letter. "Did you read it? That's why I stayed with Johnny so we could fix the Polaris for free."

"Good for you. Know what time it is?"

He shook his head and looked at his wrist.

"Where's your watch?"

"Well . . ." Leo scratched his head. "Sort of paradox."

"Not for Volkswagen. Just got off the phone with your boss. He wondered if you were sick. Told him you had trouble with your buggy and that you would reach out to him soon."

"It's not a buggy, but thank you. And Marlo? Did he come yesterday?"

Angelina shook her head, rattling her lock beads—her gesture of disapproval. "Why so eager? You don't play at home that often."

"Because I don't like to play with an audience."

"You're so fond of this man. See it all over you. But why does he pick you up on horseback?"

"I've told you. He's a ranch hand. And learning the piano calms my soul."

"Why do I feel you're not telling the entire story?"

Leo shrugged. "Because you only listen to R&B."

"And this Fred guy. When are you going to meet him?"

His heart skipped a beat. "Fred . . . ?"

EPILOGUE: NEW BEGINNING

"You wrote you would visit him this afternoon."

"Wow . . . well, yes. Actually, I found him. Mom, can you believe it?! He was at Gump's Gas. His parents own the place. And what's even more miraculous,"—Angelina took a step back—"he forgave me! No financial demands. They even offered to pay for my fuel from this day on." Angelina raised her eyebrows. "Mom, I wish you were there—or . . . that I could tell . . . it was simply heavenly."

"Heavenly . . . ? Your new karma is paying off. One less burden on our shoulders."

"It isn't karma. You know, I can tell you why I'm so joyful, if you really wanna know."

"Please do tell."

Leo glanced at the sailing clouds. "Dear Jesus, help me," he said silently. Immediately, Leo felt this was not the time. He grabbed Angelina's hand. "It's just . . . so amazing to be forgiven."

His mother smiled. "Thank goodness you're safe and sound." She rubbed his shoulder. "At least some good came out of it. But remember to show your poor mommy some mercy too."

Leo nodded, pondering everything he couldn't say. "Yeah . . . I'll be better at that."

"Your mother needs more assurance than a handwritten letter when you suddenly stay with a stranger overnight. What if Johnny was crazy?"

"I hoped you wouldn't notice, but he actually boiled me in his wizard's pot all night."

She chuckled. "Maybe that would have been better—something decent might have popped out of the cauldron. Okay, Smarty. Do what you have to and get to work. Fun's over."

He followed his mother up onto the porch. "Ah, I forgot," she said. "Ken called last night. He couldn't reach you. He wondered if you can come over during the week—Leo, that young man's becoming a real ladies' man. Even through the phone, he's charming."

Leo rolled his eyes. "Mentioned UniBrace, didn't he?"

"Uni-what?"

"He's leading a new student initiative. *Unite to Embrace and Face to Change.* Guess I'll head over."

Hip-hop music bounced off Leo's chest as Angelina opened the door. For the first time, he cringed at the lyrics.

His mom moved to the staircase, cupping her hands around her mouth. "Gem'! Turn that down! Guess who's here!" The blasting bass faded.

Everything in the living room—except for the flat-screen—bore the marks of being secondhand, and a discolored upright piano stood under the staircase leading to his and his brother's rooms. Yet Angelina's aesthetic touch, her handpicked wildflowers, the antique-looking furniture, and the view over the vast caramel-colored plains, always gave Leo a mythical feeling of unexpected adventures when he entered.

"What?" a voice shouted, and a door upstairs squeaked. Leo's sixteen-year-old brother, with a blond half ponytail and freckles on his nose, froze in the doorframe. Shorter and more strongly built, his brother wore a Captain America T-shirt and ripped jeans. "Leo!" He ran down the stairs in his flip-flops and knocked the air out of Leo as he clasped his arms around him.

"Gemini, bro! Careful. Man, that hurt."

His brother let go, gazing at him with his green eyes. "Sorry. What happened to ya?"

EPILOGUE: NEW BEGINNING

"Long story, but the Polaris is fixed. Seriously—feels like forever since I left."

Gemini's face lit up. As Leo's closest friend, his brother seemed to know what was happening in his life without him telling. "Leo, something has happened to ya. Haven't seen that smile in ages."

Angelina laughed. "See?! Leo, you've been exposed. What's up?"

"Guys, give me a break. I'm just happy to be home."

Gemini elbowed him. "When you're ready . . ."

Leo gave him a firm look.

"Sorry."

Angelina's phone rang from their old-fashioned kitchen.

Leo sniffed the air. Tobacco? He stepped closer to his brother and sniffed again. "Gemini," Leo whispered. "Are you giving in to the Yazzies' pressure?"

"What do you mean?" His brother backed up and Leo followed.

"You know what I mean. I can smell it." Gemini's eyes widened and Leo lifted his finger. "Quit it. You hear me, bro?"

Gemini swallowed. "Why suddenly so—?"

"Leo," Angelina whispered, pointing frantically at the phone pressed against her shoulder. "It's Christopher."

Leo closed his eyes. A shiver rushed through his body, every hair on his back standing on end. "Help me, Jesus."

His mom handed him the phone, nodding firmly.

He groaned. "Hello?"

"Hey, Leo! Staying out of trouble lately?"

"Oh, hi Officer Archer. So sorry I hung up on you. I didn't expect a check-in yesterday, and I was awfully stressed, so I—"

"Can't you hear I'm funny?"

"Funny? You're never funny, sir."

His Probation Officer sighed heavily. "Rub it in—not even my wife gets my jokes. Seems like I'm the only one who thinks I'm hysterical."

"Yes, sir. That might be true, sir."

"I called Volkswagen this morning. Why are you not at work?"

"I'm so sorry, sir. My Polaris broke down in the middle of nowhere and I got home minutes ago. I'm on my way." The probing silence only emphasized Leo's shaking hand. "I mean . . . the oil filter leaked, and I needed help from a local to fix it. My Mom and brother can confirm I've been gone until now." Still silence. "Forgive me, Officer Archer. What shall I do differently next time?"

The officer exhaled. "Are you planning to work ten hours the rest of the week?"

"Yes, sir. Anything that makes you happy, sir."

"Have to say, Leo, I like your tone. You sound more upbeat than a week ago. Take this day off, help your mother clean the house, and start afresh tomorrow. Deal?"

Leo released his breath. "Yes, sir. Thank you, Officer Archer. So . . . can I still drive in the desert?"

"Honestly, Leo. Sometimes I wonder how guys like you ended up on probation the way you did. Yes, of course you can."

"I . . . I never wanted—" A soft click. Leo lowered his hand and stared at the fluffy rug.

Angelina took the phone. "I'm sorry, honey."

"He gave me the day off," Leo said, heavyhearted.

A hand touched his shoulder, but Leo stepped toward the stairs. "Need some space." Their silence betrayed their grief as

EPILOGUE: NEW BEGINNING

he ascended to the second floor, entered his room, and locked the door to his cave.

Sunbeams filtering through the closed red curtains dyed the motorsport posters, his bunk bed, a dusty desk, and a bookshelf. Leo let down his backpack and slid against the door, dust swirling from the carpet. Above his head hung a poster of Jesus caressing a lamb.

He rubbed his forehead with his palm, inhaling with a staggered breath. To deflect the searing pain, he read his letter, a few hot drops hitting the paper.

Sunday, July 26, 2020

Hi Mom,

Just so you know it's me: I've memorized all the WRC podium finishers from the year 2000 until today, and I'm a useless cook. I know receiving this old-school letter is nerve-racking for you, but please cancel any search-and-rescue operation. I'm doing perfectly well. Just had an oil leak after I hung up with you, and my phone died. I can't drive anywhere, but amazingly, a kind local guy saved my day. Please don't panic, Mom. His name is Johnny. He's a Christian and kind of Amish. A good man—the friendliest man on earth, actually. He knows how to fix my leak and will get the stuff first thing in the morning. With his help, I can drive home without using my insurance.

I know you're freaking out and want to pick me up, but Johnny has already provided food and steaming tea. I'll stay with him, fix the leak tomorrow morning, and be back before work starts at lunchtime. Camping is my standard out here, so Johnny's place is luxurious in comparison. Really no need to get me. Thanks to Johnny, I don't have to pay to fix the Polaris.

If you read this letter before Marlo comes, please tell him I'm sorry I couldn't reach him to cancel the lesson. Tell him I'll call him when I get home.

Last thing. I bumped into a gentleman and offended him. Truly, I feel so bad about it. When I get home tomorrow, I have to google his name or company and drive to his place right away. Feel it's urgent to bury the hatchet. His name is Fred Waylon. Just want to ask for forgiveness. As an adult, I gotta take responsibility for my actions, you know, and not run away from my mistakes. I'm telling you now, so you have time to process and don't have to yell so much when I get home. Love you, Mom. I know you just want what's best for me. You're a fantastic mom.

EPILOGUE: NEW BEGINNING

Leo,

PS. Johnny isn't into technology but has a friend who seems to be going down to Arizona and can deliver this letter.

Leo dragged himself up and slumped into his chair before his study desk. From a drawer, he got a calendar, a photo with torn edges, and a jar of paper bits. In the photo, he was grinning, wearing his Volkswagen motorsport outfit and holding a bronze medal on the podium of The Parker Youth 1000 Race.

He crossed off July 26 on the calendar and grabbed the photo to tear off a piece, but stopped. Leo touched the jar and turned toward the poster of Jesus. Quickly, he put it all into the drawer, opened his new journal, and wrote.

Monday, July 27, 2020

Jesus loves you. Focus on this. Don't look back either, but forward. Do you remember what Johnny tried to teach you? It's big. Bigger than your past! The Divine Calendar is God's plan for unfolding history, ticking down to when Jesus comes back. The Derailers want to stop the flow of history and forever postpone His return. You are in the middle of this. This is your new life.

Leo closed the journal and stood up before Jesus. From his pocket, he pulled out the last vial and rolled it between his fingers.

"Lord, I miss Johnny. I feel—attached. I think You left some of my soul with him, didn't You? Is he okay? I want to see him again soon."

Dimmed sunlight danced on the poster.

"And Jesus, what about Spooky? Was anything he said actually true?" A gust of wind tapped sand on the window and the house creaked. "Okay. I shouldn't think about this. But why, Lord? Why did Johnny call me Leonyx? Sounded like *Lennox*— I like Leo more."

Jesus' gentle eyes rested on the lamb He embraced. Leo put his fingers to his lips and touched his Master's heart.

Kneeling before the window, Leo drew the curtains aside and squinted. He placed the holy water on the sill next to a cross and lit a candle. The majestic Agathla Peak soared above him, its shadow almost reaching their property. He had read Scriptures that called God "my Rock"—for Leo, a crystal clear metaphor.

He opened his canister and unrolled the Legend, flooding his room with bright blue rays and flickering shadows. The eight symbols around his soul hid behind a dark blur, and only the Crevice Dweller symbol on the list of descriptions remained visible—Johnny was somewhere far away.

His soul's core had absorbed the cross-marks left by Jesus' whip. Compared to some hours ago in the bathroom at Gump's Gas, the light in his center, mind, hands, and feet shone stronger, and the glow had expanded. Could his first Chosen Steward mission not only have released Proto-Life to Fred and his parents, but to him as well?

EPILOGUE: NEW BEGINNING

Leo closed his eyes. "Jesus, I won't shut my heart from You anymore. Like a little flower that opens when the sun shines to show You its beauty, let Your face shine upon me and let my heart open up for You."

Something flashed in his face. Red beams radiated from the exact midpoint of his soul. "Jesus, now I realize who Your servant was. Again, Lord, I accept Your invitation."

In the deepest core of his soul, a red cut emerged. "You're different from everyone, Jesus. I trust You, but I'm so scared. But I want—I want You to see this wound. And to heal it."

Reaching under his bed, he pulled out a chest, rolled the combination lock, and lifted out a framed photograph from beneath silk fabrics, gloves, jewelry, and big sunglasses. Leo didn't know how long he stared at his handwriting at the back of the frame.

> Leo + Sandra Halona
> December 9, 2017 – January 24, 2020

He placed the photo, taken from a riverbank, on the windowsill. Leo and a Navajo girl with brown curly hair held hands, laughing, both wearing motorsport caps and holding paddles. "Sandra . . . forgive me."

Tears dripped in the waving crimson light. "King Jesus, I'm ready. I want a new beginning. I won't run away this time."

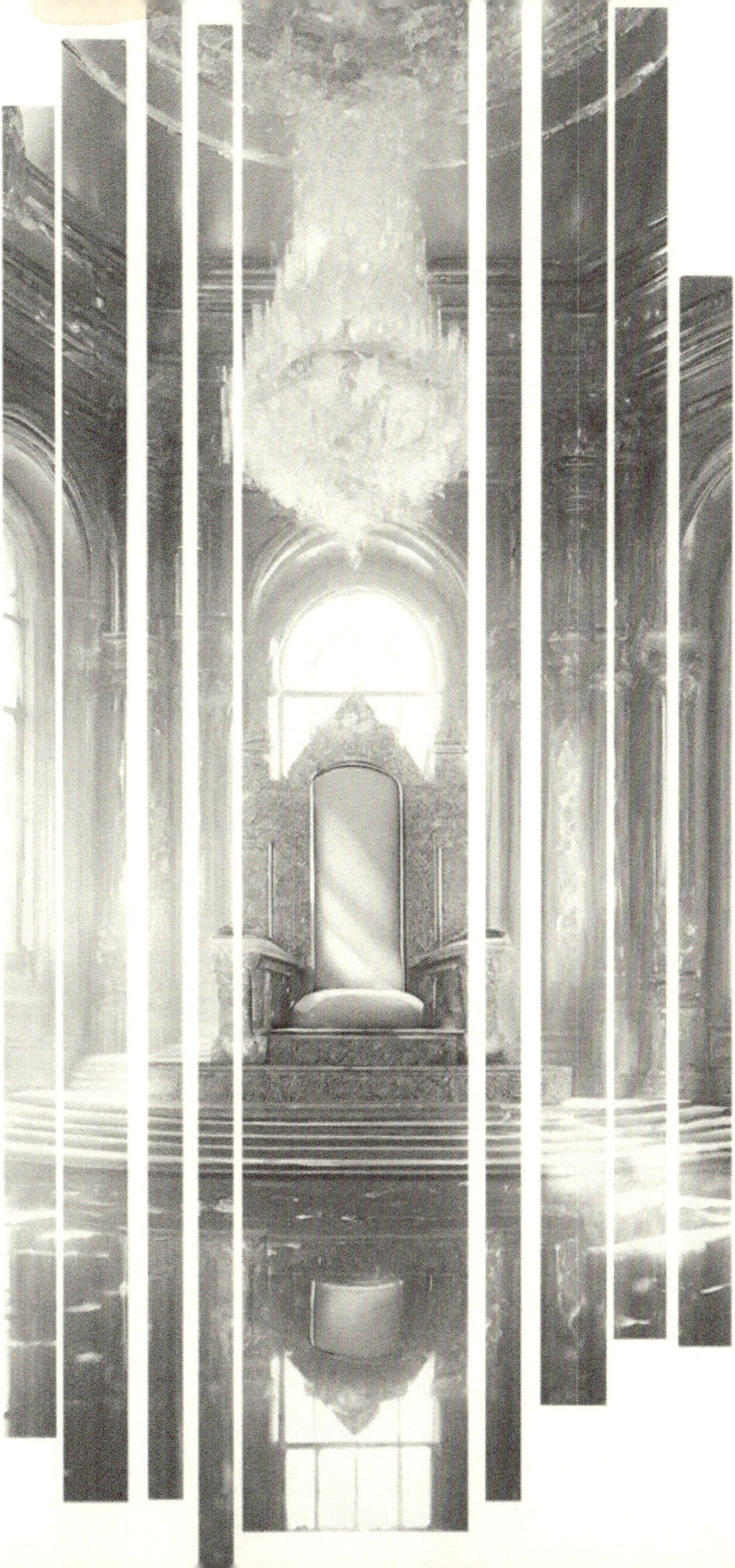

ACKNOWLEDGMENTS

This story exists because my spiritual father diligently passed onto my monastic community and myself his rich experience of the ancient mystical wells of the Early Church. This novella is based on theologically sound mysteries particularly relevant to us in the twenty-first century. I honor my abbot and his close circles of monastic disciples for years of uncovering ancient truths and passing them onto our wider spiritual community and eventually to you, dear reader. You and the Lord Jesus Christ are the reasons I write.

Many thanks to all the members of my monastery and my wider spiritual community for your love and support, which allowed me to write. I'm especially indebted to the senior monks for their teaching. A special thanks to the editor and proofreaders who helped bring this novella to life. Also, a heartfelt *thank you* to those who helped me with the website, design, publishing, and promotion. Emilia, Aquila, Athanasia, Abigail, Elishewa, Jonathan, Elizabeth, and Zachariah, the investment of your skills means more to me than you know.

I owe my writing skills first to God, then to author Jerry Jenkins. His patient mentorship made me into a professional writer. And I will never forget thanking Annie Sellman, Carla Gayle, LoraLee Kodzo, Lynne Jordal Martin, Quentin Guy, and Robin Albritton for companionship, feedback, and inspiration. You are all so precious to me.

AUTHOR'S NOTE

Exclusive Bonus Material

Access exclusive bonus material through this hidden link: fatherelisha.com/JohnsCanyonRoad

- A video where I share:
  - The story of how I came to faith.
  - How God called me to write.
  - How the idea of this story evolved.
  - A concluding prayer of blessing over you.
- Wallpapers of Leo, Johnny, Miryam, and Fred.
- Images of scenes from the novella.
- And more . . .

Find *The Legend of the Divine Calendar* on paperback and Kindle e-book on amazon.com.

All income from this novella goes to my monastery and supports me in writing more stories and other content available on fatherelisha.com.

What Was Your Experience?

Your feedback and experience from reading this book is a most precious gift for me. What did you like or dislike about this story? What touched you emotionally or spiritually? Any other feedback? Please email hello@fatherelisha.com with your review. By doing so, you grant me permission to anonymously post your review on fatherelisha.com.

If you liked this novella, will you help spread the word by posting your review on amazon.com or sharing this story with a friend?

Delve Deeper on fatherelisha.com

- Be inspired by weekly insights into the Divine Calendar of the Early Church as I guide you through the Seasons of Salvation on my blog.
- Go deeper into your spiritual life through the tracks of fiction, non-fiction, or as a spiritual seeker.
- Ask me a question about the spiritual life, or read the answers I have given to others.
- Sign up for updates about new content.

May we glorify Jesus Christ and honor Him through our lives. To God be the glory. "Let a man so consider us, as servants of Christ and stewards of the mysteries of God." (1 Cor. 4:1)

ABOUT THE AUTHOR

"Let me take you on an intriguing journey and expand your vision for life."

Under the monastic name of Father Elisha, the author is an Orthodox Christian monk with an expertise in Christian spiritual life.

The author became a Christian in 2008 as a 22-year-old, and from 2010 to 2016, he served full-time in the evangelical mission Youth With A Mission (YWAM) in Europe, Africa, and the Middle East. He professed his monastic vows in 2016 and moved to a monastery in the US, belonging to the Eastern Orthodox Church, where he currently resides with other monks.

Father Elisha's experience as a missionary in the Western Church and monastic insights from the Eastern Church have given him a heart for every Christian, regardless of denomination. After having spoken with hundreds of strangers from other worldviews in the streets, in coffee shops, on public transportation, and elsewhere about Jesus Christ, Father Elisha respects every person whom he believes God made in His image.

The author writes mainly inspirational fiction interwoven with spiritual mysteries to inspire a deeper love for God, regardless of the reader's faith in Him, and to broaden the vision of one's life. He also writes nonfiction and spiritual expositions on his website.

Visit the author's website or social media to delve deeper, get in touch, and be notified of new publications.

fatherelisha.com

HiFatherElisha

Made in United States
North Haven, CT
24 September 2024